THE LAST FLIGHT

SEBASTYEN DUGAS

URBANUM
ÉDITION

GET TWO FREE BOOKS

Get two FREE short novels from this author. Discover two of his book series by visiting Sebastyen's website.

Download them for FREE by subscribing to Sebastyen's newsletter by clicking on this link:

https://link.sebastyendugas.com/brevisfrontlibrary

1

─────────

Half-conscious, Alain Dupont was standing in the middle of the road, rubbing the back of his neck to get rid of the pain. The day was wonderful, with the sun glowing in the clear blue sky.

Behind him, a disturbing thick smoke was coming out, which was not good news. He staggered away as quickly as he could toward a blurred shape ahead. His whole body hurt as if something had crushed him dozens of times. His ears were stuck, but he could still hear muffled noises in the distance. Screams.

Terrible, spine-chilling screams.

He struggled to stand but needed to find out where the screams were coming from. He couldn't help it. He couldn't stand it. He closed his eyes, then opened them wide, trying to see clearly. It was all blurred. He couldn't make out what was in front of him, and he didn't know why.

There was a huge yellowish thing in the distance resting in an alarming fog, yet he couldn't figure out what it was. There was complete silence all around, except for laments that became less audible as the clock ticked down. He moved toward the sounds, doing everything in his power not to stumble over obstacles on the way, despite his blurred vision.

The strong afternoon sunlight was not helping his eyesight. His pupils were burning, and he didn't have his sunglasses on. He turned back to look at the black smoke rising into the sky and noticed that it had become thicker and flames had erupted. Even though he couldn't see very well, there was clearly something wrong with this picture, and it didn't look promising. One thing was sure; he had done the right thing by stepping away from the fire.

The screams went on. He focused on the yellow blob and quietly approached it. If he could see what was going on, he could at least do something. He tried to put the pieces back together as he walked straight ahead. He didn't know what he was doing here, what had happened to him, or why his sight was so fuzzy.

Then, an explosion came from behind, startling him, and he spun around. He saw the blaze forming a huge nightmarish sphere and gasped as he realized he could have burned to death if he hadn't had the presence of mind to get away.

He took another long breath to build up courage, to get a better sense of what lay ahead. He kept moving toward the mass, then noticed some motion further down to his right. He instinctively backed away, fearing what it might be. Perhaps it was a strange animal or something that meant him harm.

He had a severe headache. Massaging his temples, he watched a beige, black, and gray body move in the ditch to his right like a wave of a thick liquid or a vast tide of motley shapes. He thought the screams came from this slimy lump. He knew he shouldn't, but he couldn't help it; he had to get a closer look at what it was. He was unsure if anyone was in danger or in need of help. The people responsible for the screams that had plagued him since he woke up.

He slowly put one foot in front of the other and moved carefully toward the shapeless mass. The screams were fading away, giving way instead to a haunting wail. He rubbed his eyes with his fists, hoping to improve his vision, but it was no use. He figured he probably suffered a blow to the head, which was why his eyesight was impaired, probably a concussion.

If anything, he was making this up.

He moved closer, feeling an overwhelming pull grabbing him low and dragging him toward the misshapen blob. The yellowish mass to his left had sharpened to the point where he could see a flickering glow, like a railroad crossing. There was no fire or smoke around, only that damn wrapping mist and undefined moving form.

The yellow shape was half tilted down toward the ditch, and Alain Dupont foresaw moving shapes at the other end. He concluded that there was something in the ravine and that the mass was partially buried in the abyss. The other half was lying somewhere on the road. The shadows were growing more active, but still, he couldn't see what it was.

Dupont squinted again to spot something but failed. He needed to get closer, even if every fiber in his body was urging him to run in the opposite direction. He walked quietly, cautious of what he was about to encounter. Then he heard voices, high-pitched voices he could not understand.

"Is anyone there?" he asked, feeling ridiculous for even expecting an answer.

As expected, no one responded. Only muffled and alarmed whimpers.

He was now a few feet away from the lump and flinched as a shadow crept by his foot. He tried to move back, but a powerful grip grabbed his ankle like an enormous and insatiable boa constrictor.

Panicked, Dupont stumbled as he sought to free himself. He pounded the slender shape with his left heel but had little leverage in his stance, especially since he was right-handed. Moreover, his left leg was clumsy and inaccurate, causing him to strike mostly wide of the target.

He clutched the ground so hard that his fingernails popped off in his grip. He was dragged toward the mass and screamed for help. Unfortunately, there was no one around to assist, and he was left to his own devices. His right leg came dangerously close to the ravine. He began to yell like crazy to get out of the clutches of this monster.

His body went limp as he realized what was holding him so tightly: a huge hand with sharp claws encrusted in his ankle. A green, scaly beast was at the other end of this long limb. No sound came out of Dupont's mouth, even though he was screaming his lungs out. What he saw was horrible. How could it be? God, no!

All those eyes staring at him, begging.

He screamed, and this time he thought his soul was slipping away. It was too awful. He could not hold on any longer. Then, in a sharp movement, the huge hand pulled him into the ravine.

Sweating in his bed, Alain Dupont had screamed like a madman. He was disoriented. His mind was numb from the horrific images he had just seen, but he was safe and sound, sitting by himself in his huge queen-sized bed. The room was so dark he couldn't see two inches in front of him.

Why did these same images keep coming back to his mind? It had been a long time since he had had this nightmare. He thought he was cured. He assumed that all the therapy sessions had paid off. Yet it devastated him to see that this was not true. Those horrible visions were still lurking in some dark corner of his mind!

He wept with dejection. Would he never come out of it? Would this hell for which he had paid an enormous price would linger for the rest of his life? Would he ever live a normal life again? Was he doomed? It was everywhere. No matter where he was, he couldn't get away from it. Even at work, he occasionally noticed shadows passing by him. He realized it was just a figment of his imagination, but it felt so real. Fear gripped him, and he could not focus anymore. A long series of sleepless nights ensued, Alain, dreading to fall asleep.

Never to dream about this again.

After a couple of angsty seconds trying to find his place in space and time, he sighed as he recalled he had to join Myriam, his new girlfriend, in the vice capital the very next day. She had already been in Las Vegas for almost a week for a conference in her field of expertise. The plan was to join her for the last day of the conference, and then they would spend some time exploring the city. His flight was scheduled for later in the evening, and he felt anxious just thinking about it. He couldn't delay it any longer. This was the moment of truth.

His eyes grew accustomed to the darkness, and he made out some shapes around him. He lit his bedside lamp and glanced at his suitcase, which was already done and set by his bedroom door. He folded his flight clothes and laid them on the captain's chair in the room's corner. His flight was scheduled for 6:30 p.m. this Friday, a beautiful April day. At least, that's what the forecast predicted.

Alain Dupont's heart was still pounding from the nightmare, and he was still on alert as if something horrific might still happen.

Even though he was alone in his apartment and well into his thirties, he felt like he was three decades younger. He felt scared like a child, afraid that a monster was lurking in the dark, ready to jump out from under his bed. Thankfully, he was no longer eight years old. He could reassure himself and put things into perspective.

Of course, he was alone in the apartment. He had locked all the doors. His senses were on high alert because of his bad dream. Whatever fear he was feeling was bogus, fueled by his imagination. None of it was real. It was just a dream. A dream that felt damn real, but a dream nonetheless.

He was about to drift back to sleep when the floor creaked next to him. He turned over quickly and turned on the light once more.

Nothing.

He went back to sleep shaking like a leaf. He felt utterly vulnerable to an evil spirit with sinister intentions.

"You are alone, Alain. You are all by yourself. There's no one in this damn apartment."

He would probably settle down and go back to sleep if it weren't for the intense impression that something was watching him at this very moment.

2

———

Dupont was busily unbolting a loose part from a car wheel axle. Renowned as an expert mechanic, he had converted to mechanics after working as a truck driver for over a decade. He was more at ease in this role surrounded by people than on his own in a ten-wheeler. As a result, he had chosen not to renew his driver's license for years. Instead, he relied on cabs and Uber services. Otherwise, he rode his beautiful hybrid electric bike to get some exercise along the way.

"Frank, can you help me?" he shouted at a man in his fifties who was talking to another colleague.

Frank Dubord quickly ran to join him. If Alain Dupont was asking for help, something was wrong. Alain was self-organizing most of the time.

"Hold that while I get to the back."

In a concerted effort interspersed with muted grunts, Alain grinned as he heard the gratifying sound of the part coming off the axle.

"Thanks, buddy."

"Anytime, Alain."

Dupont wasn't scared to get messy with grease and dust. He wasn't intellectual and loathed pen-pushers as he sarcastically called the nine-to-five office workers. He believed that manual work was the only genuine work. He was critical of those who slaved on a computer screen and then crashed watching TV for the rest of the day. What a shitty, boring life! When he would come home, Alain really had a sense of fulfillment. He enjoyed finding solutions to troubles in cars assigned to him. He liked to keep his customers happy, to have them back on the road with a vehicle in perfect condition. That was his daily motivation.

Then he gasped as a toolbox crashed to the ground. He bent down to see what had happened and who had caused the commotion. He was disappointed to see that Pascal Monette had gotten himself into trouble again. Monette was shouting loudly and cursing like a maniac, risking that customers from the lounge would overhear him. Alain quickly headed to him to calm him down before the boss noticed. Monette already had a bad rap with him, so he could only make it worse.

"Keep your voice down, Pascal. Clients can hear you."

"I don't give a damn. Who put the toolbox in the way?"

"Do you want Marchand to go at it with you again?"

Monette stared at Alain Dupont, furious, but had no answer. He knew he had pushed his luck with Jean Marchand, the garage owner. He was one slip-up or misplaced comment away from being out of work. It was his fear. He struggled to keep jobs and couldn't afford to lose this one. Alain could smell booze coming from his young colleague's breath.

"Damn it, Monette. Have you been drinking again?"

"Only yesterday."

"Stop bullshitting me. You reek of booze from a hundred yards away. It wasn't just yesterday, for sure. Stop lying to me."

Monette considered disagreeing, but Alain Dupont, the recovering alcoholic, was trying to help him. Alain knew all the lies he could come up with. He had taken him under his wing, but Monette was too immature to appreciate it.

Even if deep down he would have liked to grab the opportunity Dupont was offering, he couldn't. Drinking was too good for him to pass up. He couldn't imagine sipping water or soda in a bar or with his friends.

He was bored when he was sober. He was the most annoying person you could meet. When he was drunk or stoned, or better yet, both at once, he was the life of the party. He would make his friends and the ladies laugh and sometimes even end up with one girl. He was ashamed of his filthy one-room apartment, but it was all his shitty job could provide.

"Excuse me, Alain. It's just that—"

"If Marchand sees you like this, you're screwed. Go home; I'll take care of it; I'll improvise. But for the love of Christ, don't be drunk tomorrow. I won't be there to bail you out."

"What do you mean?" Monette asked, having forgotten entirely about Alain's evening trip to Las Vegas.

Dupont watched Monette put on his jacket and discreetly exit the garage. He then walked into the boss's office.

"Hey boss, Monette went home. He was really not feeling well."

Jean Marchand sighed as he sank into his chair.

"Drunk again, I guess?"

"No, he only has a sick stomach. He was hunched over, and I told him to go home. He'll probably feel better tomorrow."

Marchand watched Dupont for several seconds, wondering if his trusted employee was being truthful or if he was covering for his colleague once again. He then smiled courteously and told him to go back to his station.

Dupont went back to the garage to pick up the tools Monette had knocked over and went back to his client's vehicle to finish the job. Frank Dubord came to meet him.

"Why are you covering up for this asshole?"

Alain kept removing the bolts from the drum brakes on the old car he was fixing.

"Because he reminds me of myself at his age. I was as dumb as he was and as lost. I wish someone had given me a chance instead of being abandoned. It would have kept me out of all kinds of trouble. So if I can keep him from living through the same crap I've been, then that would be worth it."

"You know you can't help him unless he admits he has a problem," Frank retorted in his English, tainted with a thick Marseille accent.

Dupont looked at the grey-haired, copper-skinned man with a slight smile. The old man was right. Alain was probably wasting his time. But he couldn't resolve to let the young man wither away without trying his best. If there was a slim chance of saving him, then it would be worth it.

Especially with what his own addiction had cost him. Years of trying to get his life back on track, patching up the scraps of his existence. At the bottom of his decline, he thought he'd never make it.

He looked at the huge Bridgestone clock on the garage

wall. Only one hour left, and his vacation would begin. But instead of being thrilled to join his sweetheart in Vegas, he felt anxious as he realized he was heading straight for the airport.

He had only been on a plane once when he was a teenager, and it had scared him to death. One engine had burned out, and the plane had to make an emergency landing on a small island near the Caribbean. The oxygen masks had fallen down, and he still vividly recalls the panic that prevailed at that time. He remembers the distraught flight attendant who was looking at him, looking for comfort in his eyes, feeling like they were going to die.

Dupont had vowed never to board a plane again.

But his new girlfriend, Myriam, was a travel enthusiast, and she had asked him to travel with her a few times, but he had always refused. They had been together for six months, and he felt Myriam was second-guessing their relationship because of this.

There was no way she would stay with someone who couldn't fly, who was afraid of flying. It would be an insurmountable obstacle. Traveling was her greatest passion in life, so much so that she would rather break up with a man who couldn't keep up with her trips. No relationship was worth sacrificing the opportunity to see the world. It was non-negotiable.

Since they both had their own apartments, it would be easy to break it off. But that was the last thing Alain wanted. He finally felt he had met the right girl. He was happy with her. Things were simple. She had accepted his past, even though she came from a conservative family, and the most dangerous thing she had done was to get a speeding ticket in a school area.

Despite their contrasting personalities, they were a perfect match. He didn't want to ruin that, so he had to overcome his fear of flying. Myriam traveled a lot for business and was at a professional conference in Las Vegas. Alain would then join her to spend the next week with her in a city he had never been to before. Some of her colleagues had planned to stay there for a second week also, and Myriam had plans for the group.

Alain didn't like to mingle with strangers. He wasn't much of a talker and was extremely shy. He was an incurable introvert, so the mere idea of spending time with a bunch of people made him very anxious.

But he would do it for Myriam to show her he was dependable. He needed to overcome his irrational fear of flying. After all, plenty of people flew every day without a single incident. Professional and amateur sports teams flew all the time, and there was hardly ever a catastrophe, accident, or even a minor mechanical problem.

Frank had told him it was by far the safest form of transportation. Safer than a car or a bicycle. He regularly traveled to the south of France to visit his remaining relatives. Moreover, Alain always wanted to explore the Las Vegas casinos. His favorite movie was Oceans Eleven, both the Frank Sinatra and George Clooney versions. He wanted to see the Bellagio and the Paris Hotel and sit at a few gambling tables. He loved to bet. That was his weakness, especially Black Jack and Texas Hold 'em poker.

He tried his best to keep his fears at bay, but his nightmare from the previous night popped into his head. He wondered if one day he would quit having this awful dream and stop hearing the screams. He still felt like he was being watched, like the night before. He still felt it right now, at work.

It was hard to describe. He didn't feel like someone was watching him, but rather it was a thing, an evil spirit. An immaterial presence. Something that didn't exist but wanted to harm him. He glanced behind, but nothing was wrong, only colleagues working like relentless bees.

Dupont sighed and got back to work. First, he had to finish replacing the brakes on the damn thing. Then he would head quietly to the airport. Now, if he only could get rid of that lump in his stomach. If only he could get rid of the dread creeping up on him more and more.

3

———————

Alain Dupont was anxious. He had not been feeling well since he got to the airport. The mere sight of the crowded airplanes at the boarding gates was scaring the hell out of him. This trip was a bad idea; he felt it already. He wasn't even sure he had the strength to keep his word to Myriam. Failing meant the end of his relationship with her for all intents and purposes. He would never travel the world with her if he could not fly. And she had clearly stated her passion for traveling. They were an impossible match.

He had sat down at the Archibald Brewery restaurant, relaxing with a few soft drinks to complement his beef tartare. He was jealous of the surrounding people, so relaxed and happy at the idea of leaving for a distant location. How much he wanted to be like them, to be free, to feel this carelessness, this abandonment at the idea of flying, but he was terrified. He was sweating profusely to the point where he could feel his back totally soaked as his body fluids drenched his shirt.

He needed to relax. There was no sense in being so tense.

He kept telling himself about the sports teams flying all the time, that it was safer than driving, and another preconceived phrase that a friend had used to comfort him. He would have much preferred to go by car, but since it was about forty uninterrupted hours of driving, he would only have a day or two to enjoy Las Vegas before he had to ride back the other way.

It was ridiculous.

He had found the woman of his dreams, but she had to be a travel freak. Why hadn't he found a partner who was as afraid of flying as he was? Why hadn't he found a woman who would have been happy with car rides in Vermont or Florida?

His beef tartare was delightful, although he had eaten better ones. He had purchased a bottle of sparkling water since he didn't drink alcohol anymore. Booze would have settled his nerves and even helped him sleep during the flight, but it would cause far more problems than it would solve. He knew this, and he rarely fooled himself.

But the idea of dozing through the flight was very appealing. It would really be ideal. Dying in our sleep was what we were all hoping for, right? Inert body, consciousness escaping into an imaginary world as we are close to death when we sleep. We might as well be halfway there if we were to kick the bucket. The voyage would certainly end more quickly. He would travel back with Myriam so she could take his mind off it. Or maybe if the flight went well, it would cure his fear of flying. Or at least lessen his worries.

He spotted a well-known journalist chatting with a woman two tables away from him. She was either his daughter or his girlfriend. She was much younger than him, but she was an adult, so it didn't matter. It felt funny to see a scribe he cherished reading in person. He would like to chat with him and tell him how much he enjoyed his work, but surely everyone else was doing the same. He would be just annoying nobody to bother him rather than let him be. Then he reflected on his flight. He had arrived at the airport very early, hoping that being here would help him unwind, that looking at all these tourists who didn't care about flying would make him feel at ease. But when he saw his watch showing there were only two hours left before his flight, he became dizzy. Hell, he'd never make it.

"Are you okay, sir?" the waiter asked.

"Yes, I'm fine," said Dupont, trying awkwardly to sound upbeat.

Even the journalist was looking at him from afar, sensing there was something wrong. Dupont nodded at him, but he didn't reciprocate. Alain looked away, embarrassed. His hair was soaked as if he had just stepped out of a shower.

He paid his bill, grabbed his wheeled suitcase, and headed for the nearest bathroom. He rested his hands on the sink and stared at his reflection in the mirror. He was as pale as a ghost, and his eyes were red as if he had smoked three doobies back-to-back. There were huge, sweaty rings on his pale blue shirt.

People looked at him funny, and it was totally justifiable. He looked like a guy about to have a heart attack. He shut himself off in one restroom cabin and closed the door. He opened his spare suitcase and happily found a black t-shirt and a towel. He wiped his body and sponged his face and hair. He removed his shirt and put on the T-shirt. The softness of the dry fabric on his skin cooled him down. He wrapped his shirt in his towel and stuffed it in his suitcase. Now people would at least stop staring at him. He didn't like to draw attention, so he did everything in his power to blend in with the rest of the crowd. This was more like it.

He walked out of the bathroom, but as he turned the corner, he collided with a large man. The man apologized, but when he realized who he was dealing with, his face turned red with anger, and his features became threatening.

"Watch where you're going, you idiot."

"Sorry, I didn't see you," Dupont said to avoid a clash with the burly man.

The other guy stared at him for a few seconds that seemed like minutes, as if he was considering what to do with him, and he hurled another muffled insult, then jostled him again with a shoulder blow before rushing into the bathroom.

Alain Dupont's heart was pounding, and as someone who hated confrontation and violence, he couldn't be more alarmed. He had been terrified and dejected to be sweating again. He grabbed the handle of his suitcase and hurriedly made his way to gate sixty-four, where he would later catch his flight. He figured that by walking quickly, the air would either dry him out or keep him from sweating. He would be happy with both.

The first gate he passed was number five. He sighed as he realized he'd have a long walk to get to his. He just wanted to sit down, put on his wireless headphones, listen to some relaxing music, and close his eyes. Many people were in his path, making it difficult for him to move forward, as he typi-cally walked with his head down, staring at the floor. He never looked people in the eye when he walked. He fixed his eyes on the ground as he made his way as best he could to his destination.

No, really, he didn't want to attract attention.

He stopped near gate thirty-six to buy a coffee. It was inconsistent with his wish to sleep during the flight, but he needed a little pick-me-up and craved a good latte. He finally arrived at gate sixty-four, where half the seats in the lounge were taken. His legs went limp as he saw the enormous frame of the Airbus 320 standing still in front of the immense window of the departure lounge. An accordion-style walkway was already glued to the side of the aircraft, and a forklift was sliding heavy wooden pallets full of gear and supplies through another door.

Alain couldn't fathom that such a gigantic piece of scrap metal could fly, especially considering the weight of over three hundred people and all the luggage. He sat down on a chair along the aisle and closed his eyes. He took deep breaths, and his heart rate finally began to drop.

The boarding attendants had not yet arrived at the reception desk, and the flat-screen TV behind it displayed the flight number, AC810, the destination, and the expected takeoff time. They still expected the flight to be on time. Alain Dupont would have liked the flight to be delayed to give him more time to talk himself into it. Or better yet, that the flight be canceled to give him an excuse not to join Myriam. That way, it wouldn't be his fault and buy him a little time. Obviously, she would suggest that he take another flight, but he was enjoying the simple thought of a cancellation. Except that it was just another one of his whims; the flight would take off.

His hands were shaking as if he had Parkinson's, and he could feel the back of his neck moisten. "Get a grip of yourself, for heaven's sake," he thought. He grabbed his headphones out of his suitcase, fired up his classical music playlist, and placed the headphones gently on his ears. He smiled as he heard the first few notes of Beethoven's Opus 62 Coriolan. He loved classical music. He got that from his mother, a talented pianist who had raised her children instead of chasing her dream of becoming a famous classical pianist. She said she didn't have the talent anyway, but Alain didn't believe her. She had a perfect pitch and played beautifully.

Shortly before she died, she had requested some of her favorite Beethoven and Mozart CDs at the hospital. Then she was gone, just like that, siding with the two great maestros in the afterlife, surfing the tracks they had written two hundred and fifty years earlier.

Dupont had read that Beethoven had dedicated the Coriolan opus to Heinrich Joseph von Collin, an Austrian author he was fond of, around 1807. Alain tried to picture Von Collin's reaction the first time he heard the grand master's melody in C minor. How beautiful and touching it must have been. Dupont opened his eyes and immediately lost his smirk when he saw the hulk of a man he had had a run-in with in the bathroom earlier. He was scrutinizing him with a simmering rage.

"That's my seat," he shouted in a sinister tone.

Dupont frowned but quickly realized that the man was looking for a confrontation, and he had no intention of taking the bait. He complied.

"I'm sorry. I thought the seat was free."

"It wasn't, you fucking asshole."

Dupont didn't know where all this guy's hostility came from. He rarely triggered this kind of nasty reaction in people, so what did the unknown guy want from him? He grabbed his things and took off quickly amidst the man's verbal abuse. Except that now, there were no more seats available.

Dupont was careful not to stare anyone in the eye and slowly made his way to a wall further away, then sat down on the floor and put his headphones back on. He sighed deeply and noticed a child of about five years old looking at him with his soft eyes. Alain smiled shyly at him, and the child smiled back. The boy was wearing a three-piece suit with a tie. This kind of attire in young boys gave Alain the creeps. He didn't know why, but it scared the shit out of him. Who dressed their kids like that for a flight, anyway? It was crazy.

Alain suddenly freaked out, thinking that the madman could be his potential seatmate. If he was, Alain would get out of the plane. It was out of the question to suffer the wrath of this behemoth, visibly antagonistic against him for some reason. Sure, he had bumped into him, but that happens all the time. At the very least, he could understand that he was angry back then. But to still be angered almost thirty minutes later? That was very odd.

The child was still staring at him with a straight face. Dupont looked away, but the boy moved as if he wanted to stay in his field of vision. When Dupont looked to his left, the kid stretched his neck to his right. Alain looked at him again, perplexed, and the boy sat down, keeping him in his sight. Alain smiled again. Then he felt a shiver of fear cut across his spine.

The little boy smiled back with a blood-soaked mouth and sharp tiny teeth.

4

Leaning against a metal column near gate sixty-four, Michel Madison was enjoying a raspberry danish while watching people waiting for their flight. He loved to watch people's behavior from the sidelines.

Humans fascinated him both in all their graciousness and in all their shortcomings. He had already noticed a few prominent figures, but he watched them all. He treasured individuals who explored the globe. It was a trait he valued highly. He liked curious people willing to take risks to broaden their minds and soak up bits of culture.

He was particularly drawn to a few people, but mostly to Alain Dupont, the one this entire trip was about. Madison watched him with amusement. The guy was about to have a panic attack or just outright collapse. He was like a deer in the headlights in the center of a highway. He was totally out of his element, out of his comfort zone.

Madison was also intrigued by another, taller, bigger man who was clearly upset and about to explode. Michel

Madison crumpled up the wrapper of his danish and threw it into a nearby trash can. He smiled at a woman who glanced at him and then walked up to the furious man.

Another taller, bigger man who was clearly upset, about to explode, also intrigued him. Michel Madison crumpled up the wrapper of his pastry and threw it into a nearby trash can. He smiled at a woman who glanced at him and then walked up to the furious man.

"Excuse me, what time do you have?"

The man looked at him sternly, about to retaliate aggressively by pointing to the screen ahead displaying the time in large letters, but when he saw Madison's face, he kept quiet.

He looked round at the others and then back at Madison, who was still waiting for an answer with a smile on his face, even though they both knew it was rhetorical. The big man's face softened, and he folded his legs, opening the magazine he held on his thighs.

Madison glanced at Alain Dupont sitting on the floor at the other end of the lounge, his back against a wall. Totally appalled.

He then tiptoed to the large window overlooking the plane he would board in a few moments with all the people sitting in the lounge. "What a majestic aircraft," he thought. He had seen many of them in his long life.

He felt as if he had witnessed the birth of humanity unfold before his very eyes. It had grown so much; it was amazing. But humanity was a lot of work for him, plenty to work with.

Madison opened his backpack and pulled out a bottle of water he had purchased, along with his pastry. He took a sip of the cold liquid and immediately felt refreshed. He sat on the edge of the window next to other people who had not been lucky enough to get a seat.

A woman in her seventies tried to sit next to the window but couldn't. Madison stared at a man who had laid his backpack on the seat next to him until he finally noticed. The two stared at each other for a few seconds before Madison turned his eyes back to the old woman and again to him. The man, too, stared at the woman, then stood up to talk to her. He whispered something in her ear, and she smiled. The man went back to his seat, glaring at a grinning Madison. He grabbed his backpack and dropped it between his feet. The lady walked over and sat down in the now vacant seat. She thanked the young lad, and he smiled at her.

Madison looked back at Dupont, who did everything humanly possible not to look at anyone. He didn't notice that Madison was checking him out. Then he got up and disappeared into a further bathroom, in a corridor between gate sixty-four and sixty-six.

Dupont had walked by the large man on the way. Madison had noted no shift in the latter's expression. Dupont had glanced at him with concern. Madison laughed dryly and saw a woman wearing an airline uniform moving to the reception desk behind the podium.

It was a woman in her mid-forties with dark, curly hair to her shoulders. She seemed to be on her game despite her rugged exterior. Madison stood up to stretch out his legs and greeted her as she walked by. She looked up and smiled. Madison wondered what Alain Dupont was doing in the bathroom while everyone was about to board the aircraft.

He sensed Dupont was deeply agitated, as if he were fighting an internal struggle. Like the frequent flyer he was,

Madison had often seen this fear upon the faces of those who dread flying. This was clearly Dupont's deal. Madison had to find a way to get him to come back and chill out.

Because if there was one thing he knew for sure, it was that Dupont absolutely needed to get on that plane.

5

———

Dupont had splashed chilled water on his face in an adjacent bathroom. He had to calm down because everything was going haywire. Obviously, his mind was spinning stories, making him see things that weren't there. The touch of the fresh water had startled him and brought him back to his senses. He chuckled when he saw his gloomy look in the mirror. "Yeah, you're really falling apart, man," he thought. He settled down at the little café close to his gate, where he could hear the call to passengers. He did his best not to mingle with the crowd because it made him feel uncomfortable. He didn't know why, but it was as if an immense strain weighed on him when they were around as if an imminent danger was hovering over their heads. At least, it was hovering over his.

He refrained from looking at the stalled planes outside, fearing that his mind would spin again, and closed his eyes for a visualization exercise.

He pictured himself getting into the plane, looking straight ahead. He envisioned cheerful people enjoying themselves, calm and affable, not worrying about the possibility of a mid-flight disaster. With their huge smiles, he could see the flight attendants welcoming him on board and showing him to his seat. Then he gasped and screamed out loud.

He looked around and noticed that people were staring at him. He attempted a smile by tightening his lips to reassure them. For a moment, he sensed that the faces of the passengers in his visualization were twisted, whereas, in the beginning, they were soft and welcoming. But, then, their eyes had become black as night. It was as if all these heads had split off from their bodies and had ended up in a mass grave, staring at him with their dark eyes, imploring his help.

Like in his nightmare.

It was a sign. There was no way he could get on that plane. He had never experienced such a horrifying feeling. Something bad was bound to happen to him, that was for sure. His legs were shaking, and he couldn't do anything about it. Ambient noises filled his ears. He could only hear the bass tones of voices, like whispers that echoed loudly.

Dupont put his hands over his ears and scanned the place, looking for a way out or something to soothe him and bring him back to reality. Something that would shut off the horrible images his brain was throwing at him. Then, he grabbed his wheeled suitcase and dragged it behind him to head back to his gate. A lady dressed like an airline employee was working on shuffling through papers. He reached for her.

"Ma'am, I'm sorry to bother you, but I can't take this flight. Is there any way to get my luggage back?"

The woman stared at him as if he were asking the stupidest thing ever enunciated in human history. Yet it didn't seem like an unusual request. Surely he couldn't have been the first to have a last-minute impediment.

"It's too late to remove any baggage. They are already on the aircraft, and we will start boarding in the next few minutes.

"You don't get it. I can't get on this plane. I need my luggage back."

The short woman with dark curly hair hardened her gaze, taking care to speak carefully in order to make herself clear.

"Sir. It is out of the question to take out your bag. If I can guarantee you one thing, it is that it will make the trip to Las Vegas. It's up to you to decide whether or not you'll go with it."

Dupont was very agitated and had resumed sweating profusely.

"I have some personal things that I absolutely need, ma'am. You don't understand; I must at all costs—"

She raised her hand.

"I'm going to ask you to move to the side, and I'll proceed with the boarding. Then we can file a claim for your bag to be on the next flight from Las Vegas to Montreal. You can pick it up when it comes back."

"Will that be today?" Alain Dupont said in as neutral a voice as possible.

The woman sighed as a colleague arrived at her side. Upon seeing Dupont, the tall, slender young man asked if everything was all right. The woman glanced at Dupont, who stared down.

"Everything is fine," she said after a few seconds. "I'm going to check for the gentleman when the next flight is scheduled so that he can get his luggage back. He says he can't get on that plane."

She typed on her keyboard at a prodigious speed with a clenched jaw. She could have done this without this inconvenience. She had better things to do than to worry about a man in his early fifties, unable to handle himself. She informed Dupont that the return flight was set for the next day in the early afternoon. He could then pick up his bag at the carousel assigned to that flight. She asked him once again to step aside, that she would take care of him next.

Dupont complied and sat down on one of the blue leather benches in the lounge because several people had gotten up to line up for boarding. Dupont thought it was strange since everyone had already secured a seat, but he didn't have time to think about that. He needed a solution to his problem, and sooner rather than later. That he couldn't get his suitcase back immediately was a major concern. First, his coat was in that bag, and his laptop was also. He only had his iPad and his e-reader with him.

He looked at the people in line, and his eyes met the big man, who still looked like he was pissed at him for a perfectly harmless incident. Shit, couldn't he just leave him alone once and for all? Why was he picking on him, for heaven's sake? He had apologized a thousand times since he shoved him.

But what surprised Alain Dupont the most was several people behind this guy stared at him with just as much resentment. This asshole must have told anyone who would listen about what happened. Boy, the drama people could make out of nothing, for crying out loud. It wasn't like he'd tried to kill the guy or called his mother names.

Dupont glanced behind him to the back of the room

where he had been sitting before. He gasped when he spotted the little boy in the suit in the distance, kneeling in his seat, gazing at him. What the hell was this nonsense? Although they were two distinct problems, Dupont saw similarities.

Two people physically distant from each other and obviously having no connection could not wish him harm simultaneously. Unless the large man had been bitching about him to his parents? Of course not; that was ridiculous. The two were on opposite sides of the room.

What did the boy want from him then? Dupont had no unusual features to attract anyone's attention. He wasn't particularly handsome and had no distinguishing traits that would captivate a kid. He was a little overweight and dressed in beige clothing. Anything to stay under the radar. So why was this kid so enthralled by him? And why did he have blood in his mouth? Had he bitten himself? Did he have bad gums?

Dupont twisted as he heard the dark-haired woman call for people from business class, those with disabilities, and children to be granted priority boarding.

Dupont knew there were five zones on the plane from a sign hanging on a post delineating two entrances to the boarding station.

He looked at his ticket and realized that he was in zone three, seat 22-A.

He had requested a window seat even though he had no intention of looking out. He would panic seeing the aircraft soar through the air to the point where anything on the ground would become as small as a scale model of a city. He had chosen this seat because he wanted to lean against the wall near the miniature window and sleep. He would have previously lowered the plastic window flap so that he would not have to open it again until he reached Las Vegas Airport.

He had time to unwind as people in zones one and two took their seats, but they still glared at him. The aggressive man had already gone into the tunnel, so he wasn't sitting next to him. That made him feel better—finally, a positive first thing since his arrival.

The airline woman called zone three on the microphone, but Dupont stood still. His heart was pounding, and thoughts were colliding in his head. While, on the one hand, he thought he would board the plane, on the other hand, he couldn't see how he could. Then he thought of Myriam and felt depressed. When he thought of her, he came to believe that some misfortune would happen. Either a breakup because of his ineptitude to fly like a normal human being, or he would be trapped in this long metal tube that would launch itself thirty-five thousand feet into the air. All that remained was which poison he would prefer.

And there was that damn luggage that would only be back the next day, depriving him of his computer and other things he would have difficulty coping with. And that was if they actually sent his bag back on the next flight. What if it sat in circles for hours on the carousel at the Las Vegas airport only to end up in the lost and found? What if someone grabbed it and thought it was abandoned? Dupont realized he was biting his nails with a disturbing fervor.

What the hell? He needed to get a grip; he wasn't a child, for fuck's sake. He had always wanted to see Las Vegas; he wanted his relationship with Myriam to work and didn't want to spend the next few days waiting for his bag like an idiot.

With a gesture that took him by surprise, he got up and

stood behind the last person in line. He glanced behind him one more time. The child was no longer there. Yes, another piece of good news. Finally, it was probably his imagination playing tricks on him. He was panicking over nothing. The mind could make one believe in crazy things to protect oneself, make one believe in whims. That's what people who hallucinate must have experienced. And that probably was what he was going through; hallucinations. The imposing man was real, but the little boy with the bloody mouth? Clearly a figment of his imagination.

He handed his boarding pass to the stern-looking short lady, who glanced at him long.

"You changed your mind?"

"I did, and sorry about earlier."

She kept glaring at him, worried. She grabbed Dupont's passport and scanned it into her computer. She looked at the screen for a few seconds, then turned to him.

"You will not cause any trouble on this flight, Mr. Dupont?"

Alain frowned.

"Of course not. You really don't have to worry. I'm meek as a lamb," he said, forcing a smile that wasn't reciprocated.

"Have you been drinking?"

"No," Alain replied, surprised by the question.

"Are you sure, Mr. Dupont?" the woman said in a dry tone.

"Of course, I'm sure. I drank sodas and a bottle of carbonated water, that's all. I've been sober for years."

The woman still looked at him, alternating between the passport and himself.

"You know that aviation laws are tough on anyone making a mess during a flight?"

"I swear I won't cause any trouble. I'm going to Las Vegas to relax and catch up with my girlfriend. I plan to take a nap during the flight and wake up over there. I have no intention of stirring up any trouble."

Some people in the queue grew impatient as others switched sides to go through the young man's line, processing people faster than a cashier at the grocery store.

"Okay, Mr. Dupont. I trust you."

She scanned his ticket and gave it back to him, tucking it into his passport

"Have a pleasant flight," she said in a softer voice."

Dupont thanked her with a tense smile and walked toward the bridge to catch up with the others, sighing. He felt his legs falter again and cursed his inability to loosen up. He put his headphones around his neck and checked that his iPhone was still in his right pocket. He joined the group in the tunnel waiting to board the aircraft, and Dupont stowed his papers in his small suitcase.

Just like when he woke up the night before, he still felt like something was watching him. As if some entity was following his every move. He wasn't used to attracting attention or arousing anyone's curiosity. He believed others might sense his anxiety, and that's what was bothering them.

Dupont scanned the sea of people in front of him and saw no one watching him. He took a deep breath. Obviously, this flight was making him eager to the point of fabricating things. He had to compose himself, especially considering that he had reached the point of no return.

He was going to take this flight. He no longer had a choice.

For better or for worse.

6

———

Dupont walked quietly toward the plane's entrance. Two flight attendants checked passengers' boarding passes and showed them to their seats. Each step forward added a layer of stress. Dupont quickly glanced behind himself to assess his options but realized in a flash that the line was too long. There was no way to go back without looking like a complete fool. And still, there was that damn unrecoverable luggage to worry about.

He thought back to when he was at home, wondering if he should put his laptop in his carry-on bag or leave it in his big suitcase. Choosing the second option was the source of his concern now that he wanted to cancel his trip. He looked at the flight attendants up front and did everything in his power to stay calm. "Everyone looks composed. The crew is smiling and at peace. Pull yourself together," rolled around in his head. Still, his heart was pounding. He couldn't do a thing about it, despite everything he might say to comfort himself.

Then, something unusual caught his attention. The

metal doorway leading to the aircraft appeared uneven, higher on one side than on the other. It had seemed perfectly symmetrical a few seconds earlier. Then, the two sides of the upper part widened quietly and stretched out. Dupont looked around, but no one seemed to see that. He looked back at the entryway, and it was clear as day. The outline of the opening now turned into a wide evil grin, and everything went dark. He sharply screamed as he felt a hand on his shoulder.

"Are you all right, sir?"

A peaceful-looking man was scrutinizing him with a worried look. Dupont nodded, attempting a grin that looked more like a scowl, then ran his hand over his sweaty forehead. He gazed toward the aircraft's opening again, and its outline was once again symmetrical. There was only one plausible explanation for what had just happened: anxiety was making him hallucinate. He took a deep breath as he closed his eyes. "Come on, damn it. Snap out of it."

He was next to board the plane and handed his boarding pass to the flight attendant with a shaky hand. The slender, pretty woman with long blonde hair neatly tied in a bun lost her smile as she saw his name on the ticket. She stared at him sternly and curtly told him where his seat was. Then she looked at the person behind her and regained her good humor. It was nothing to comfort Dupont, who wanted things to get back to normal as soon as possible. He was sick of people reacting strangely. He wanted things to run smoothly; he needed reassurance and support.

He guessed that the flight attendant had treated him with contempt because the clerk in the lounge must have told them about his odd behavior before in the lounge. She must have warned them he might cause some trouble and to keep an eye on him. The flight attendants were probably already on alert. Dupont thought of all this while waiting for the man in front to put his bag in the upper compartment. He took one more deep breath; the passenger glared at him.

"Are you kidding me with the sighing? Can I take time to put my stuff away, asshole?"

Alain Dupont's eyes widened, unsure why this man was acting aggressively for no reason. He made sure not to show any hint of animosity when he replied.

"Sorry, I wasn't sighing. I was taking deep breaths because I'm nervous, that's all. I'm afraid of flying."

"Well, no reason to piss everyone off."

Dupont thought it was better not to retort and looked away. He crossed with a woman sitting to his right who was watching him with an equally belligerent look. Actually, all the passengers were staring at him sourly. As he turned to look back, he noticed that even those behind him were treating him the same way, as if they all wished him harm.

Dupont became dizzy and leaned on the bench to his left, much to the chagrin of the occupant. The guy who had just finished putting his things away sat down furiously and kept staring at him. Dupont shrugged him off and moved forward to catch up with the other group in front. The print-outs under the baggage compartments showed 16 A-B on his right and 16 D-E-F on his left. Only seven rows to go before his. He felt his legs shaking so much that he thought he would collapse. Could these people move any faster, for heaven's sake?

A quick flicker drew his attention near one of the luggage compartments. Underneath some suitcases were four aluminum baseball bats. Dupont frowned, shocked that people could bring these long, heavy objects that were of no use on an airplane flight onboard. Worse, one could use them as weapons. Why not check them in and put them in the cargo hold? But since he was not familiar with flight procedures, he thought it might be normal. He glanced around at those already seated to his right and resented that they were also staring at him. It made no sense at all. Why did these people he didn't know hate him so much? What did they want from him?

18 A-B.

He thought he would never make it to his seat at this rate. He scanned the passenger area for the first time to assess the aircraft's layout. There were three rows of seats in total. One with two seats on each side, along the windows, and then a row of three in the middle as far as the eye could see. So much so that it made Alain dizzy. How could this heavy plane fly with all those people on board? The plane he had taken when he was young was smaller. In his memory, there were two rows of two seats in total. This aircraft was monstrous. It was physically impossible for this behemoth to rise to thirty-five thousand feet in the air. And yet, it would.

20 A-B. Only two rows left.

A huge guy blocked his path, and Dupont patiently waited for him to finish taking his things out of the bag he had stuffed into the luggage compartment. He stared down at the ground so as not to look him in the eye. Above all, he didn't sigh. Then the guy turned, and Alain felt his legs go limp. It was the man from the bathroom. Wasn't he supposed to be in business class? He had entered with the first wave of passengers. Nothing made sense anymore, but it didn't matter since the man's face went from neutral to furious, quickly reddening as if he was about to explode. Dupont wanted to take a step back, but someone was standing in his way. He figured this man would not hurt him on this plane, in front of all these people. Still, he was terrified. Alain hadn't been in many fights in his life. He had done everything in his power to avoid confrontations in the past.

"That's right, look away, faggot," the hulking man said with an evil smile before sitting down.

Alain had stayed silent. He didn't mind being called names; it was harmless. It was not something that bothered him, and he would prefer an insult to a punch in the face.

Once the aisle was clear, he moved on. He was so eager to sit and get on with things. He wanted to vanish into his seat and be forgotten. When he reached 22 A-B, he was relieved that his seat was located right next to an emergency door. Myriam had given him good advice. It was worth paying a premium to have more leg room. He put his bag in the luggage compartment above his head, keeping his headphones and his e-reader with him.

Since he had everything in hand to enjoy the trip, he settled into his seat and looked out the window. The weather was great; it was 6:31 p.m., and it was still daylight. It felt like a blessing after a winter where the sun set around 4 p.m. every day for months.

His flight was about six hours long, but he would make up three hours of jet lag when he arrived in Nevada. That meant he would be on the ground just before 10 p.m. Myriam would wait for him at the hotel's main bar. Then they would go out to eat with two of her colleagues before hitting the hay. Alain wished he hadn't agreed to this since he expected to be exhausted once he got there. But if he dozed off a bit on the way, maybe he could recover enough energy to get through the evening without looking like a zombie. He had trouble sleeping in transport, but he had everything he needed to do so: a small blanket resting on the back of his seat and eye patches provided in a clear cellophane bag.

He was still contemplating the exterior when he felt a presence on his right. A middle-aged man with an agreeable face looked at him with candor.

"Hello, this is my seat. You see? 22-B."

Alain wondered why he showed him his pass; he would have taken his word for it. He had no reason to argue. But he was glad that his seatmate was a seemingly nice guy. Hopefully, he would not be gossiping the entire flight. Alain hated small talk. Especially since he wanted to sleep and recover all the energy he could muster. He hoped he wouldn't have to tell the man to let him be.

The man extended his hand.

"Pleased to meet you. I'm Michel Madison."

"Alain Dupont," he replied, putting his hand in his.

Madison's hand was rough, and the grip was so strong that Alain Dupont winced. He hated it when people crushed fingers when shaking hands. For God's sake, weren't they aware that this was not the way to introduce yourself to someone? That it made a bad first impression! The same goes for limp and clammy handshakes as if you were grasping the leg of a dead chicken.

Alain stared into the man's eyes and was mesmerized by his azure eyes. An electric shock went from his arm to his lower back, making him jump and release his grip. Alain looked at Madison, who was still smiling and watching him as if he could read his soul. Dupont felt overwhelmed by his presence and stature, as if he was entrenching him in a corner, dominating with his majestic aura.

"Well, my friend," Michel Madison said as he turned to open the bag he had slipped under the bench in front, "I feel like we are going to have a very interesting flight."

This comment took Dupont aback. Why would he say that the flight would be interesting? Who said that? A flight was a flight, right? But Dupont didn't care.

Michel Madison ogled the surrounding people, smiling and introducing himself. This guy was much too gregarious for Alain's taste, but he had to admit that he was facing his own social shortcomings, which had plagued him all his life.

Alain Dupont was dark-haired, with brown eyes and a receding hairline, much too prominent for his liking, even if he was good-looking. Madison had brown hair with greying temples, and, apart from his piercing blue eyes, he was quite tall, although not a giant. A lanky, long-distance runner type.

The man was the complete opposite of Alain Dupont, both physically and personality-wise. But Dupont couldn't help but be disturbed by what he had felt when he greeted him.

How cold his hand was!

7

———————

Myriam Gagnon sipped a cosmopolitan martini at the Paris Hotel bar in Las Vegas. She had just finished her last day at a conference on information technology sales. Finally, she was getting the hang of it, a week of listening to people talk about many interesting topics. Except that it required an incredible amount of concentration, a quality she lacked in every circumstance.

Her mind would sometimes drift for long minutes, only to realize that she had missed a significant portion of the speaker's words. She needed to make a concerted effort to grasp most of the matter, to take notes.

Her bosses had invested a significant amount of money in educating her so she would have a head full of useful ideas for the company. She at least had to force herself to soak up as much information as possible. Let this trip bring value to the organization. She worked as a sales representative for one of Canada's big technology companies and was proud to have worked there for twenty years. She was roughly halfway through her career, and it all worked out the way she had planned.

This was far from the case with her love life. She was thirty-eight and still not in a long-term relationship. She had no children and felt her biological clock ticking, reminding her that time was running out if she ever wanted to start a family. At this point in her life, she was debating whether she needed to have kids. She was fine on her own, just thinking of herself and moving ahead in her career. But she couldn't imagine spending the rest of her life without offspring, either.

She had just met a nice but troubled man—a very pleasant but taciturn mechanic. An opposite personality from her own, as she was outgoing and appreciated the company of others. It's said that opposites attract, but for her, Alain Dupont was mostly a physical and not a psychological journey. He was a wonderful, handsome lover and looked ten years younger than his forty-one-year-old self with his slim, trim body. He wasn't massive like a bodybuilder, but he had noticeable muscles.

Besides, she hated those steroid-induced narcissists at the gym. Suffering from early baldness, Alain had a face that was both rigid and vulnerable. Myriam didn't want to admit it, but her maternal instinct drove her to save him from his misery, to put him out of his nightmare. She wanted him to be happy, to live a good life finally. She wanted to embrace him and reassure him that things would be okay now that he was with her.

He could soar.

In the past, she had fallen for guys similar to her, often met on the job. It never worked out for long, so much so that

Myriam resolved to be daring. She aimed for a companion who would not belong to her environment, a man who would be more hands-on than intellectual—a man from another social class. This was exactly what Alain was; a mechanic who was earning a good living, even if she made much more money than he did; a rather quiet man, less extravagant, less flashy.

He was attractive, but he didn't care for himself to the point of smearing his face with a night cream before bed, getting his teeth whitened, or working on his tan. He was raw, straight out of his cavern, a far cry from the shallowness of his exes.

That's what she liked about this guy, a real man. Not an alpha male, but a guy in the simplest definition. The kind who could work with his hands, hard and with the sweat of his brow. Above all, who had no desire to steal her night cream.

She assumed her fashionable side. She talked about other people's superficiality, but she was equally guilty of it. She wore subtle makeup to highlight her features; auburn wasn't her actual hair color, and these weren't her real nails. But she thought it was normal for a woman to put on all these gimmicks. It worked for her since she was easily attractive to the opposite sex, even if they were more interested in banging her than building something serious rather than getting to know her.

That was the type of men she attracted, guys who would relish adding another beautiful woman to their trophy case. That's why she was attempting to change fundamentally. That's why she was experimenting to see how it would work with Alain. Sure, she stood out with her long, fiery hair and endless legs. But she wanted more than surface commitment. She, too, wanted a mate who loved her for who she was, not only for her looks. Of course, she wanted her man to think she was pretty and desirable, but she also wanted to be recognized for her personality, joie de vivre, and wild side. Indeed, beauty is nice, but it's ephemeral. She knew she was getting older, and she couldn't overlook those wrinkles in the corner of her eyes when she laughed. People told her this was part of her charm, but Myriam feared growing old and no longer turning heads as much as she did now.

So yes, time was running out.

Nevertheless, she knew that her relationship with Alain Dupont was at a crossroads. For if she was agreeable to many aspects of her future husband, there were some things that were non-negotiable.

Like hygiene, like the manner in which he treated her, but also a man of the world who loved to travel, who wanted to explore the planet. She had a globetrotter's soul and was searching for a travel partner. So much so that things had almost flipped the day he talked about his fear of flying. He had never traveled in his life, except by car or on organized bus tours.

She didn't want to sound elitist, but the notion of several people piling into a coach bus to go to New York seemed preposterous. Especially since it would take less than an hour to get there by plane, to each his own, she thought. This was not what she was into.

When she asked him to come to Vegas, she had to make a firm stand. The answer was to be yes, or their relationship would fail. She loathed ultimatums, but she had little time to waste. Either he was going to be that globetrotting accomplice she so hoped for, or she would keep on searching. She intended to make at least three to four trips a year and more once she retired. She wanted nothing to do with a man who would be a hindrance or who would let her go on a solo adventure. She wanted to travel the world with her lover, not with strangers, and certainly not by herself.

She checked her watch; it was 3:46 pm. Alain would arrive in a few hours and start their one-week vacation together. She had already booked a couple of Cirque du Soleil shows and a Golden Knights game since Alain was a huge hockey fan. She had targeted a few restaurants she wanted to check out and had planned a trip to the Valley of Fire with some colleagues and their spouses. They, too, had stayed for an extra week to enjoy the city and what it offered. Alain's tacitness bothered her a little, and she hoped he would blend in with the group and that everyone would have fun. It was difficult with him at times, and she had mentioned how important it was that he could socialize with a minimum of decorum.

Really, this was the ultimate test for them. If Alain overcame his phobia and attempted to be pleasant with others, then that would be a sign that it might work.

Otherwise, she would move on and contemplate doing what her friend Sylvie did, being single and artificially inseminated to have twins.

Myriam would have her mind made up soon enough.

8

Alain Dupont grabbed his armrests right after the captain announced they were the next to take off. The plane had been taxiing to the runway for about ten minutes. Dupont's heart raced each time the plane stopped, only to relax when the plane started moving again. Dupont's armpits were damp, and he hoped his deodorant would hold up with all his being. He realized he had been clenching his jaw for several minutes now and attempted to relax his jaw muscles.

Because if he kept clenching them so tightly, his teeth might shatter from the pressure. Alain had read somewhere that the human jaw was as strong as a gorilla's but that their teeth could not withstand the pressure without eventually disintegrating. He had read that humans had a biting capacity of about sixty kilograms per cubic centimeter. Far from the bite strength of a lion with its four hundred kilograms per cubic centimeter, or that of a crocodile, reputedly the strongest in the world, with its two thousand and forty kilograms per cubic centimeter. Alain had a photographic memory that helped remind him of this kind of triviality, only useful to impress guests at well-drunk parties.

"Are you okay?" Michel Madison asked, startling him a little.

Dupont's nerves were on edge. He absolutely must find a way to calm down. He nodded.

"You're as pale as a ghost, my friend," Madison said with a sneer.

"I'm not super into flying," Dupont replied, staring straight ahead.

Madison chuckled again.

"That's an understatement," he said. "You know, the crunch comes during takeoff and landing. So therefore, in a few minutes, you will know your fate."

Alain looked at him furiously. Madison kept his wide smile. He patted his arm and promised that he had nothing to fear. He had a much better chance of dying in a car than on a plane.

"Did you know that according to estimates, you would have to fly every day for five hundred years before you crash on a plane? I don't know about you, but I don't plan to live that long."

Although Alain Dupont just wished Michel Madison would shut up, he felt a little more relieved by this statistic. It was quite revealing, and he remembered reading somewhere that flying was much safer than traveling by bus, car, or boat. His hands loosened their grip slightly. But he clenched them again at the sound of the jet engines firing up. This was it. There was no way back. He had no control over anything anymore. The die was cast. His life was in the pilots' hands and in a few thousand screws that would do their best to hold the fuselage together.

He felt the plane speed up and rise into the air. He closed his eyes and clenched his jaw even tighter; everything was going to be all right. It had to be. If it did, then maybe his fear of flying would go away, and he could do whatever travel Myriam wanted in the future. This thought brought a slight smile to his face. How he wished that were true. He was so awake that he could hear every bolt on the plane working hard to hold the entire airframe together. He kept his eyes closed, as he did whenever someone forced him onto a roller coaster. He had never had the courage to watch the ride as others did. He thought that if he didn't watch, nothing bad could happen, and he noticed he was doing the same thing on that plane. It was as if the denial was shielding him from the repercussions of his decisions or actions. But life had proved him wrong more often than not; that no matter what he ran from, consequences always caught up to him.

Dupont heard a small bell and opened his eyes. The seatbelt pictogram over his head had gone out. Then the woman in front of him unbuckled her belt and turned to look at him, smiling. Dupont also smiled, but the woman lost her cheerfulness, and her face darkened. The man next to her did the same as the passengers in the row to Madison's right. They were all watching him as if Dupont had just said or done something horrible. Alain felt the panic increase tenfold in him just as his eyes met those of Michel Madison, who was staring at him with his shit-eating grin. Then, he spoke a word that Dupont failed to grasp. He asked him to repeat.

"Boom," Madison reiterated.

Dupont didn't get it. Boom what?

Madison shrugged. His eyes turned harsh, but he was still smiling. He said "boom" again.

"What do you mean, boom?" Dupont said angrily.

Michel Madison pointed to the window and said the same thing again.

"Boom."

Dupont lifted the panel of the window and stared at the wing beneath, then a huge fireball appeared, shattering the engine. Alain Dupont stiffened, clasped in place by his seatbelt. The flaming turbine detached from the wing, and Dupont saw it fall as if in slow motion, pulled down by gravity. He screamed as he turned his face away and realized that everyone was standing, staring at him with impassive faces.

"We just lost an engine," he shouted, not understanding why everyone else didn't perceive the precariousness of the situation. Instead, they just stood there, silently staring at him.

Dupont looked at Madison, who also stood up to stare at him.

Alain struggled to unbuckle his seatbelt. He was stuck.

"Help!" he shouted to the flight attendants standing near the cockpit, hoping one of them would hear him.

"Help, we've lost an engine. Tell the captain we've lost an engine."

Then he recalled a news report pointing out how a jumbo jet like the Airbus 320 could fly with only one engine. Surely that explains why he was the only one panicking. He stopped trying to unbuckle his seatbelt and watched the others stare blankly at him. What did they want from him, for heaven's sake? He didn't know them except Michel Madison, which was quite recent.

"Why are you all looking at me?" he asked in a muffled voice.

No answer, except a slight murmur from the back of the

plane, but he couldn't make out anything. Then the passengers' lips moved more and more as the hubbub grew louder, like a long lament. And he felt panic down his spine as he recognized the passengers were all saying the same word, in the same key, in tune.

Boom.

Dupont freaked out, totally baffled by what was happening, and plunged straight into a vivid nightmare. Why were they saying that word again? The answer to his question came almost immediately when he heard another blast from the other side of the aircraft. His eyes widened as a fireball emerged from an opposite window.

"Oh my God," he whispered.

He pulled on his seatbelt, which still wouldn't give way, as the passengers approached him, chanting boom, boom, boom.

"What do you want from me? We are all going to die, don't you understand?"

Then all the passengers burst out laughing loudly at the same time with the same laugh. And repeated boom, then laughed, and said boom, and laughed alternately.

The plane quickly nosedived, and Dupont hit his forehead on the seat in front of him, still held back by that damn seat belt that refused to give way. The plane made a thud as it fell, like the sound of a missile about to hit the ground. He scanned around, screaming, and didn't grasp how the other passengers were still standing, unaffected by the centrifugal force, just repeating boom and laughing. Gravity had no effect on them, as if they were immune to the laws of physics that propelled the aircraft toward disaster.

Boom, boom, boom.

Dupont glued his face to the window and watched, helpless, as the ground approached at breakneck speed. Finally, he closed his eyes and screamed with all his strength.

He woke up abruptly, Michel Madison's hand on his arm, trying to bring him back to his senses. Alain was sweating, and his hips were aching because his seatbelt had become embedded in his pelvic bones. The seatbelt sign was turned off, and Madison had unbuckled his belt. Dupont reached out to unbuckle once again, but his hands were shaking too much. The back of his neck was soggy, and he was having trouble unlatching the belt buckle. Madison gestured to let him help. He lifted the belt buckle with one finger, and it immediately snapped.

"Are you okay, buddy?" Madison asked, looking concerned.

Dupont nodded, his mouth pasty. "I'm going crazy," he thought.

He noticed that many of the passengers were still glaring at him. He had probably been screaming in his sleep, and they were worried about him. Madison confirmed he had yelled.

"You scared the shit out of us, man."

Dupont winced and looked for an available bathroom. There was one behind them. He apologized to Madison, who stood up to oblige. Alain stumbled through the aisle to the bathroom. Just as he arrived, someone stepped in front of him and closed the door to his face. He stopped dead in his tracks to wait his turn just as his eyes met those of the little boy in the brown suit who was playing with two toy dinosaurs. He was hitting them together in a mock ice age fight. It was the same boy as in the airport lounge. The kid stopped playing with his toys and looked at Dupont, who could not help but look back at him. He felt forced to stare into his eyes as if a morbid impulse compelled him to do so.

The child smiled, though there was no blood in his mouth this time. He had short baby teeth, as one would expect from a child of his age. Dupont shivered at the boy's attire. He was terrified of these kids dressed as adults. What the hell were the parents thinking, bundling them up like that?

Then, just as a man came out of the bathroom and Dupont was about to go in, the child mumbled something as he looked at him, and it made his blood run cold. It was unequivocal.

Dupont felt his energy drain from his body, not believing what he had just heard.

Then the boy said it again, this time standing up and screaming.

Dupont took a step back. There was no more doubt. The child had just told him the worst thing he could hear at this moment.

"Boom."

9

———

Emotionally drained, Alain Dupont put on his headphones, covered his head with his hoodie, and closed his eyes. Obviously, this flight couldn't have gone smoothly; that would have been too much to ask. There was no way it could go by the book. His fear of flying wouldn't just magically fade away enough to go with Myriam on her upcoming trips.

Except that there was no problem with this flight. The problem was him and his damn obsessions perverting his mind, his fears that infested him to the point of imagining inconceivable horrors. The boy had not looked at him with his mouth bleeding before the flight and had not whispered "boom" while Dupont was waiting near the bathroom. If anything, he didn't even exist.

And once inside the bathroom, only his imagination made him believe people were banging on the door like crazy, ordering him out. His sick mind envisioned that the bathroom door had twisted and was being forced open by someone trying to get in.

He hadn't imagined his own begging screams, asking to

be left alone. So it did not shock him to see people looking strangely at him when he opened the door. He had kept a low profile all the way to his seat and ignored Madison's inquiries about what had just happened. Then he'd retreated into his silence and Black Sabbath's harmonies.

If this was all a figment of his imagination, then why was he panting, unable to keep his fears and visions in check? Why was he suffocating like a marathon runner? Why was he sweating profusely, and why was his heart beating so fast that he thought it would burst in his chest? He was like a bystander in his own demise, like in a movie when you have no control over what is happening in front of your own eyes, in your own body, or your very own head.

No matter how hard he tried to cool down, to admit that he was making stuff up, the tension in the aircraft was real; these people were staring at him, no doubt about it. He didn't make that up. So what was this all about? What did they want with him? Sure, his jitters were as obvious as the nose on his face, but that much? So much that all these people would stare at him? For this? A few people, sure. He could relate. But all the damn passengers? Didn't they have better things to worry about than a random guy who had done nothing to them? Everyone had a touch screen on the back of the seat in front with a selection of enough movies they could watch forever. Instead of worrying about a miserable guy disintegrating in his seat, they should focus on that.

He turned to Michel Madison, who was watching him with half a smile. He saw his mouth uttering words that the Iron Man song prevented him from hearing. He sighed and pulled out an earpiece.

"What's that?"

"You don't look so good."

Dupont frowned. Why did he care if he was fine or not? He was blunt.

"I'm fine, thanks."

"It doesn't look like it."

Dupont sighed, annoyed, put back his earpiece and closed his eyes, crossing his arms and settling back in his seat. But he could still feel Madison's gaze on him. He knew for a fact that he was still staring at him cockily, smiling. Every fiber in his body urged him to look at his fellow passenger again. Finally, he opened an eye and saw that Madison was still speaking to him. Alain shrugged and pointed to his ear to show that he couldn't hear him, that he was listening to music, and that he had absolutely no intention of stopping. But Madison waved him off, which irritated him greatly. He considered letting him speak for himself, to shut him down, but since he appeared to be the only one who did not have a grudge against him, he complied, although he looked irritated enough to show that he was reluctantly obeying.

"What do you do for a living?"

"I—uh—I work in a garage."

"A car garage?"

No, asshole. A space shuttle garage.

Dupont nodded.

"Wife, kids?"

"Listen, buddy. I don't really want to talk. I just want to—"

"—keep getting crushed by your anxieties?"

Dupont's eyes widened. How did he know about that? Was he a shrink or something? Of course not; Dupont was an open book. Clearly, he was terrified. Madison had simply picked up on it like anyone paying attention would.

"I'm an organic shampoo representative," Madison said to change the subject.

"And what's your name? Tyler Durden?" said Dupont, rolling his eyes.

"No. Michel Madison."

Dupont laughed as Madison failed to pick up on his Fight Club reference.

"Let me ask you some questions. I like to get to know people, and besides, I feel like I know you and don't know you at the same time."

What a strange thing to say, Alain Dupont thought. Obviously, they didn't know each other. "I have never seen this man in my life," he thought. Then he figured it would take his mind off things, force everyone else to go back to their damn touch screens, and he could finally chill out. He already felt less tense and had no horror visions since he started talking to Madison. So there was some merit to this. If talking to him the entire way would shun further psychotic episodes, why not? He said he didn't have a child but had a new girlfriend.

Madison did not respond to Dupont's polite questions and went on with his. What was his favorite food? What was his childhood like? What did he like to do for fun? All the while, Dupont glanced around and regretfully noticed that people were still casting scattered acrimonious looks at him.

He could not bear Madison's gaze. There was something mesmerizing and disturbing in his eyes. He couldn't put his finger on it, but after about ten seconds of staring at him, he had to look away. He laid his eyes on the man's left hand resting on the seat's armrest and noticed his skin's texture for the first time. It was as if his hands were older than his face.

Perhaps he'd had plastic surgery? He asked how old he was, but Madison just smiled.

"Come on, how old are you?" Dupont asked.

"You won't believe me, and besides, I'm asking the questions."

Despite his worried look, Dupont thought Madison's smile was friendly. Like an old uncle who would look out for you. People were seldom kind to him, but Dupont felt confident that if Madison didn't necessarily wish him well, he didn't wish him ill either. But then, his attention was drawn to the man's wrist, which looked like it had some kind of permanent wound. It was in the shape of an octagon, really singular for a wound or a birthmark.

"Sixty years old?" Dupont said with a shit-eating grin.

"Not even close," Madison said.

What does he mean, not even close? Dupont thought he couldn't be that off. Madison was probably between fifty and seventy. Since he wouldn't admit his age, Dupont dropped it. He wasn't particularly interested, anyway. Finally, there was a break in Michel Madison's long series of questions. Dupont sighed deeply.

"Am I boring you?"

Dupont looked at Madison quizzically.

"I beg your pardon?"

"I'm asking if I'm boring you."

"No, why?"

"You sighed."

"I took a deep breath. What does everybody on this plane have against deep breaths, for crying out loud?"

Heads turned as Dupont raised his voice a bit, but Madison remained unfazed.

"Maybe everyone here hates you?"

Dupont's blood ran cold. It was as if he was confirming his suspicions. As if Madison could see right through him. He froze, not knowing what to say. Then, after a few seconds of staring at him with a straight face, Madison burst into a thunderous laugh.

"Relax, Dupont. I'm just messing with you."

Madison loudly laughed as he watched other passengers laughing along with him. However, Dupont was not laughing, not laughing at all.

Madison laid his ice-cold hand on his. The chill on his skin startled him.

"What's going on?" Madison asked, noticing the expression on Dupont's face.

"Nothing. Except that your hand is—"

"—cold?"

Madison smiled. Dupont nodded.

"Not unusual for my age," Madison replied.

Dupont stroked his hand to warm it and frowned.

"You can't be that old, though."

Alain Dupont felt a long shiver run down his spine as he foresaw Madison's answer before it even came. Like a dreadful premonition.

"I'm three hundred and eighty-three years old."

Under normal circumstances, Dupont would have assumed that Madison was crazy or joking. But the man's face was straight for the first time since the beginning of the flight. What scared Alain Dupont wasn't the man's unusual age or that he wasn't smiling anymore.

What frightened him to the core was that his eyes had turned black.

Coal black.

Darkness black.

10

Alain Dupont was numb. This was more than he could take. The combination of the fear of flying and delusion, whether or not true, was more than his brain could handle. He seriously debated whether it would be better to give up and simply accept his fate. Go through each new supernatural episode as if it were normal—not to react, only to suffer. Even if he tried his best, he knew it was impossible to ignore the situation. The kid in the suit and tie, the aggressive man, the passengers with their acrimonious glances, the flight attendants who suspected him, and Michel Madison, whatever he was. He felt he couldn't act as if nothing had happened.

Clearly, chatting with a man claiming to be nearly four hundred years old wasn't a terrific idea, and Dupont went back to his music.

He opted for a change of tone, forgoing his heavy metal album for something lighter and happier. He had created a "bubblegum pop" playlist. That's what would stick with him for the rest of the flight. Fortunately, Madison had ditched him to talk to someone else. Alain could sink back into a world where neither the passengers nor the crew members existed.

But he was incapable of discounting Michel Madison's gloomy eyes. The two black beads that had replaced the hypnotic blue of his eyes from the beginning of the trip haunted his mind. How could a person's pupils change color so rapidly? Did his imagination play tricks on him again?

Playing along and talking to Madison hadn't kept his mind from wandering. Once again, he concluded he was making up Michel Madison's black eyes. It was the only logical explanation.

Dupont closed his eyes and was about to take one more deep breath but stopped halfway through. People were so sigh-sensitive around here that he didn't bother to take deep breaths anymore. He had to do everything in his power to keep a low profile. He checked the screen in front of him, which showed flight statistics—still three hours and forty minutes before the scheduled arrival time.

It was a long ride, but it would feel much faster if he could get some sleep. Then he would get out of that awful plane and meet up with his girlfriend at their hotel bar. It was tough to go through since Myriam would be by his side on the way back. But, he could relax knowing he would not have a seatmate pretending to be four hundred years old with eyes that would flip from blue to black.

Dupont felt someone tapping on his shoulder. Again, Madison stared at him with his ever-so-dark eyes, but this time he was smirking in a way that was more like a sadistic grimace, similar to a gargoyle's figure. He pulled out an earbud.

"I was talking to the people nearby about you. I don't

know what you did to them, but they have little love for you."

Dumbfounded, Dupont didn't quite grasp the meaning of what Madison had just told him. He wondered what perverse game he was playing, but he was definitely weird, and Dupont was getting more and more irritated by his deadpan comedy. He leaned over to check out the man sitting on Madison's right in the opposite row. The latter was looking at him furiously.

Dupont backed up in his seat, not sure what to do. What could he do? People didn't like him. It was absolutely irrational. People he didn't know and to whom he had done nothing couldn't just hate him out of the blue. Alain felt more and more disheartened, yet it was as if he was growing insensitive to his crappy predicaments.

It was obviously part of his new reality, so he might as well deal with it. However, one question nagged at the back of his mind: why was Madison talking about him to others? He probably had instructed the gentleman to pretend he had a grudge against him, to screw with him. But who does that? And with strangers to boot? What exactly was he trying to accomplish? Did Madison sense Dupont's anxiety and intend to capitalize on it? What kind of person would do such a thing? Alain acted as if he was in control of his emotions, not to play along with his increasingly annoying seatmate's shenanigans.

"People I don't even know aren't fond of me. Is that what you're saying, Madison?"

Alain Dupont had dealt with the worst of humanity in the past, so he could certainly put up with Madison's bullshit.

"It sounds like they know who you are."

"I don't know a single soul on this flight."

"How can you be so sure? Did you check out all one hundred and eighty passengers and crew members?"

"No, but—"

"Then what are you babbling about? You don't know jack shit."

Alain Dupont sighed loudly. This time, it was on purpose. He felt that his patience was wearing thin like grains in an hourglass. Yet he had boarded this metal bird with the best intentions in the world.

"There you go again with the sighing," Madison smiled arrogantly.

"Yes, you're pissing me off big time. I don't know what you're trying to do, Madison, but cut the crap. I wanted nothing from you, so just leave me alone."

Putting his headphones back on, Dupont heard the man laughing. He had noticed that Madison was leaning toward the other passengers, probably talking about him yet another time, but Alain looked out the window and closed his eyes. He needed to ignore him. This sweet-looking man was slowly turning into a bully of the worst kind.

Dupont felt looked at again and then opened his eyes. The woman in the front stared at him. She spoke words that the music filling his ears made impossible to understand. He frowned and took out one earpiece again. Except he still couldn't hear what she was saying while glaring at him. The noise in the cabin was deafening, filled with the echo of surrounding voices, much like a pub in which you'd have trouble carrying on a normal conversation. He finally read on her lips that she was angry that he was kicking her seat.

"I didn't knock on your seat, ma'am."

"You did. I can feel it. You are calling me a liar?"

Just as she finished her sentence, the commotion stopped, and one could now hear a pin drop. Dupont no longer heard the aircraft's engines. The lady was panting furiously.

"I'm not saying you're a liar. I'm saying I didn't hit your seat. So if you felt something, it wasn't me."

"It was you."

"Look, lady, I'm not a child for kicking people's seats without realizing it. I know very well that it's annoying."

An imposing man sitting in the other row stood up with rage.

"How dare you talk about children, you son of a bitch?"

All the passengers in Dupont's field of vision were now watching him sternly. His heart was pounding. Was he still dreaming? It couldn't be real.

Michel Madison waved the man to calm down and addressed Dupont.

"I told you, everyone hates you on this plane."

Dupont was about to retaliate, but he was so shocked by what was going on that he remained silent. It was the best way to defuse an explosive situation he didn't know the source of. He reached for his headphones when Madison's chilly hand grabbed his wrist.

"Oh no, now you've lost that privilege. I need to know what you did to these folks that made them hate you so much."

Dupont tried to break loose from Madison's grip, but he might as well admit an occult force was restraining him; Madison's arm did not flinch from Dupont's efforts and jerks to free himself. This man was as strong as an ox, and the look on his face was becoming more and more disturbing. There were more wounds or marks on his arm. Still in an octagon shape. What could that possibly stand for? Some tattoo depicting a scaled body? Dupont felt that there was embossment on the shapes, ruling out a tattoo as an option. It didn't seem like there were that many the first time he had looked at Madison's arm. Probably he had seen wrong.

Then Dupont let go. He might as well find out what he wanted from him. Why was he claiming everyone hated him? What was his motivation? Why couldn't he leave him alone, and why was he dragging the passengers into his deception?

"Okay, I'll play along, Madison. You want to play? Let's play."

"Oh, this is not a game, Mr. Dupont. Far from it."

The retort made him shudder. The voice hinted something else was on the menu, even more terrifying. What if Madison knew who he was? What if he wasn't there by chance? The thought of it scared the hell out of him. What if Madison was on that plane specifically for him?

Ludicrous. Once again, his mind was spinning and making up crazy things. Unfortunately, Dupont was stuck thirty-five thousand feet in the air with this madman and the passengers who, according to Madison, hated his guts. Trapped in this diabolical machine, racing toward a destination that Alain Dupont was not sure he would reach safely anymore.

He wasn't sure of anything.

Logic had turned into fabulation, and they were about to pass through the mirror altogether. White became black, and black became white. Like a film negative in which he was a prisoner, where he was locked up—the last judgment.

Realizing that Dupont was finally willing to cooperate, Michel Madison released his grip. Alain Dupont saw a flight attendant coming toward them, looking troubled.

"Excuse me, miss, may I have a vodka?"

He had quit drinking all these years, but this was too much. He wouldn't make it through what was coming up sober. He heard a voice whisper angrily, "You fucking asshole! The last thing you need is a drink." It came from a man up ahead.

Dupont plunged his gaze into Madison's ebony irises.

"He's right. Alcohol has brought you more pain than happiness, hasn't it? And to others as well."

"How the hell would you know about that, you fucking psycho? You don't know me," Dupont said, yelling.

Again, the same voice whispered, "They told us he had changed; he hasn't."

Dupont failed to grasp anything of the rant coming from an unknown figure.

The flight attendant stopped short and looked at him singularly.

"The service hasn't started yet," she said in a voice quivering with rage. "You'll get a drink when we say it's time. You got that, you bastard?"

"What did you say to me?" Dupont said, insulted. "What did you call me, bitch?"

The man sitting in front turned to him with a glint of anger in his eye.

"Say that again, and I will knock your teeth in, asshole. Come on, do me a favor and call her a bitch one more time."

Michel Madison stood up and took a step to stand in the middle of the aisle.

"Ladies and gentlemen, please stay calm. There's no need to get emotional. Our friend is afraid of flying, that's all. He is on edge. We would be, too, if we were him. Please, give him a chance to explain himself. After all, isn't that what we're all here for?"

Dupont's eyes widened. What did he mean by that?

"Sweetie," Madison calmly asked the flight attendant. "Can you please get Mr. Dupont a vodka? I swear he really needs it. And one for me too while you're at it."

The young woman's face softened, and she smiled and nodded.

"Right away, sir."

Madison stared at Dupont.

"There you go! You just have to ask nicely. That's how it works."

Dupont looked quizzically at Madison as he sat back down with a chuckle.

"What's the matter, pal? You look like you've seen a ghost?" Madison said in a calm voice.

"What did you mean by that?"

"That you look like you've seen a—"

"No, not that, when you said that you all are here so I could explain myself? To explain what, and to whom?"

Madison frowned.

"You heard me wrong. I don't expect any explanation from you."

"You did. I heard you loud and clear."

Michel Madison had a stern look on his face as he picked up the two vodka glasses from the flight attendant's hands. He emphasized his words.

"I will repeat what I said. I don't expect any explanation from you."

He handed a glass to Dupont, who put it on the shelf in front of him. Alain was starting to think he had misunderstood when Madison dismissed all suspicion from his mind by whispering,

"I can't say the same for the rest of them, though."

11

———

Michel Madison had, at last, stopped his flurry of questions. Alain had always hated the meaningless questions and candid platitudes, but he had been a good sport and had answered, avoiding giving too many details.

The questions about his relationship with Myriam had bothered him. He wasn't fond of confiding in strangers, especially not about his love life. Yet, he had done it anyway just because. Nothing was right; things were surreal. It destabilized Dupont, with no anchor to hold on to. So he did what he thought he had to do given the circumstances; he cooperated.

There was no escape, no place to hide. He had no intentions of hiding in any of the bathrooms for the rest of the trip. He couldn't dodge the other passengers' harsh glances, nor would they try to break down the tiny bathroom door instructing him out. All things considered, he felt safer in his seat than anywhere else on the plane.

He looked again at the flight display on the touch screen; they were down to the three-hour mark. Never had he wanted time to run out so badly, not even in prison. He was visualizing, imagining himself stepping out of the plane, free of the tension in that plane's dark and ominous cockpit. Free of all those people who apparently had a beef with him for some strange reason, and above all, never to cross Michel Madison's sinister gaze again. Only two hours and forty-nine minutes left, and this nightmare would be over.

"You haven't touched your vodka yet, Dupont. Don't you need to relax anymore? Is everything all right?"

Michel Madison's voice startled him.

"I quit drinking years ago, so it would be a terrible risk to soak my lips in it."

"Believe me, right now, drinking alcohol is the least of your worries."

Dupont looked at Michel Madison furiously.

"I'm sick of your nonsense. Tell me plainly or leave me alone if you have something to tell me."

Madison stood his ground.

"We'll cross that bridge when we come to it. Have a drink with me."

He extended his glass to Dupont, who sighed and grabbed his own, still sitting prominently on the beige plastic shelf in front of him. He clinked his glass against Madison's as was customary and went to bring it to his lips but stopped when he heard his seatmate's reproachful voice.

"We must look each other in the eye, Alain, after we hit our glasses together. Everyone knows that."

Dupont plunged his gaze into the man's and was overcome with anxiety. Madison's eyes were frightening, his irises now covering almost the entire surface of his eyes, like an afterlife scene. He almost dropped his glass but held back just in time. What the hell was wrong with this guy? Or was he going crazy? What if he was still dreaming? What if he was still in the airport lounge and had just dozed off?

He laid his glass on the shelf without a sip and felt tears of disbelief flood his eyes. He had reached the point of no return. It was now obvious; he was crazy. He had just sunk into pure delirium. As far as he was concerned, Michel Madison was probably a normal man attempting to save him from his delusion.

It was heartbreaking to realize that he would never make it all the way to Myriam, that he probably wasn't even on that plane. That he was, God knows where trapped in his terrors and deceptions. The presto had just blown. With his guilt and nightmares, his mind had finally reached the point where it was too much. It was to the point where he couldn't go on with this.

Yet it felt so real. The brain was an amazing device with incredible powers. Whenever he saw crazy people on TV or even after a brief stay in a psychiatric hospital to treat a severe nervous breakdown, he couldn't grasp that these people could live in an alternative world and not realize what was happening around them. Their subconscious probably knew it, as he had just figured out, but they couldn't get out of it, like a soul caught in an unresponsive body, a captive in a deep coma, a pure physical jail.

He couldn't even end his life; he couldn't end his suffering. He was forced to witness a sinister comedy in which he took part against his will. He was the main character in a tragedy from which he could not escape.

Then a powerful impulse struck him. He felt a fire growing within, and for some unknown reason, he started to laugh loudly. The combination of tragedy, doom, and ridicule made him laugh as if he had just heard the best joke ever told in the history of mankind. His eyes filled with tears as he laughed so hard, and he couldn't stop. The more he laughed, the more people around him became angry.

After a while, they stood up and walked toward him, foaming at the mouth, as he laughed out loud. His flushed face was paralyzed with laughter, but his eyes were overcome with a strong worry about not being able to recover. He couldn't possibly keep on laughing like that without something bad happening. What was going on, for heaven's sake? Would he ever stop laughing like a maniac?

Michel Madison also stood up as if to build a wall between Dupont and the rest of the passengers. He instructed them to sit down, saying that it was not the time, that Dupont was in an obvious psychosis, and this was how his brain was reacting. While sitting down, passengers hurled insults at Alain, their teeth protruding as if they were about to pounce on his throat.

But Dupont kept on laughing like a lunatic. He wished to stop because he could not breathe. Either he stopped or choked. Shit, at that moment, he realized one could die of laughter. Then Madison sat back down, looked at him reassuringly, and put his hand on his arm.

Alain had immediately ceased to laugh and had closed his eyes instinctively to shield himself from the intense sun rays burning his pupils. He was no longer on the plane. He was standing somewhere in the middle of a deserted road, but he didn't know exactly where.

He waited until his eyes stopped hurting to scan the surroundings. He didn't have to linger long. He realized where he was, and he screamed with rage. The ambient whispers confirmed he was back in his nightmare. Only it was worse than his horrifying dreams. He was standing there for real. It was not a dream anymore. He had returned to the place where his life had turned to shit. He didn't dare look around, but the smell of sulfur mixed with asphalt, charred oil, and the scent of blood caused him to collapse to his knees.

He sobbed loudly. He saw the same thick fog from which a huge yellow mass emerged, the same wailing from the ditch, the same flame coming from behind. He was reliving his nightmare from the day before. He felt as if his back was melting from the blazing heat coming from behind.

The moaning grew more persistent and deafened him to the point where he covered his ears to avoid his eardrums from bursting.

"Shut up," he said.

But the laments lingered. They seeped through his fingers to his ears and overloaded his brain with sounds he didn't want to hear and images he didn't want to see.

"Shut the fuck up," he said again, shouting.

Then Dupont felt a presence. He heard light footsteps. He opened one eye and backed away quickly, frightened by whoever was standing in front. The boy in the brown suit was staring at him with a straight face. Alain Dupont had fallen on his ass and had retreated with powerful heel blows on the ground. He was petrified. What was the boy doing here, in this nightmare? What did he want from him?

"Take my hand," the boy said in a whisper.

Dupont nodded vigorously; there was no way. The boy's face hardened.

"I said take my hand, you stupid jerk."

The voice that came out of his mouth was that of an adult. Dupont looked at the tiny hand reaching out to him, but he knew that something bad was going to happen if he touched it.

"I can't," he said weakly.

The boy lowered his arm, not taking his eyes from him. Then he smiled with a bloody mouth and shouted so loudly that Dupont fell on his side, screaming and covering his ears with his hands, but it was as if the roar was still passing through his hands and menacing to blow his brains out. And just as he thought his head might snap off his body, the child stopped screaming.

Still lying on the ground, his hands pressed firmly over his ears, Alain Dupont opened one eye and saw the child kneeling next to him, his face a few inches away from his. Then he punched him and sent him flying backward, sliding quickly on the asphalt toward the blaze that was burning away the wreckage of the vehicle he had been in a few minutes earlier.

He screamed as he crossed his arms over his head to shield himself. He felt he was going straight into the fireball.

He screamed as loud as he could, but nothing happened. He no longer felt the heat, no longer felt the asphalt mixed with the smell of oil and blood. He was sitting comfortably. He opened his eyes and saw that he had been dreaming, that he was back on the plane. Michel Madison looked at him, impassive. Two dozen passengers also watched him with inert faces, as did the two flight attendants who must have been about to lock him up somewhere where turbulent passengers were confined. Finally, he sat straight in his seat, looked at the flight attendants, and then apologized. He told them he had had a nightmare, although he doubted it was a dream. How could he possibly explain what he had just gone through? No one would believe him; they would think he was crazy. And he surely was. That was the worst part of the entire story.

He could no longer tell the difference between right and wrong. He hadn't come out of his nightmare; he was still in it. Only the setting was different but the same fifty shades of terror. No doubt, he was in full delirium. Then, if he was dreaming, he might as well swallow this glass of vodka that was still sitting on the shelf in front of him. He grabbed it fiercely and defiantly, looking at the others. He swallowed it in one go and put the glass back heavily.

"There, are you happy now?"

A man to his right hissed angrily.

"I can't believe this idiot has the nerve to drink right before our eyes. Dirty bastard."

Dupont was no longer taken aback. He suspected he had probably made up the latest sharp phrase he had just heard. He looked at Michel Madison and smiled.

"I know you only exist in my mind, like Tyler Durden in Edward Norton's sick mind. So who are you supposed to be? My alter ego?"

Madison grinned sardonically and nodded. Dupont shrugged.

"It doesn't matter. You are part of my imagination. The whole thing is fake."

Michel Madison watched him smiling wickedly for a few moments, then he opened his mouth, showing a sharp set of teeth bathed in bright red blood. He stretched his hand toward Alain Dupont, who felt his mind drift off his body as he heard him shout,

"I said take my hand, you stupid jerk."

With the same voice as the little boy in the brown suit.

12

Alain Dupont had been feeling strange things in his body for a moment. His lips went numb, and he had a blurry vision. He tried to report the problem to a flight attendant, but his tongue and jaw wouldn't obey. It was as if his muscles had fallen asleep, and worse, he could feel his energy draining away at an alarming rate. Michel Madison was watching him through his ebony eyes, smirking.

"You shouldn't have drunk that vodka, Alain."

Dupont stared at the empty glass but couldn't connect the dots. Why had he mentioned vodka? Was it so obvious that he wasn't feeling well? Sure enough, he could hardly shut his mouth completely. His lips were dazed as if he'd just come out of a dentist's appointment. He looked at Madison anxiously.

"We didn't think you'd drink it that fast. I don't know what's going to happen."

Madison turned to the person on his right, who just shrugged.

"No, we really don't know what's going to happen, but,

hey, one thing's for sure, we'll find out soon enough, won't we?" Madison said cheerfully, then laughed.

A cruel, Machiavellian laugh. It was all gibberish to Dupont. Trying to make sense of all the things Madison was saying, he hadn't noticed the needle in his right arm. Madison was pouring the contents of a syringe into it. Alain's eyes broadened, and he tried to fight back, but his body was so limp that he couldn't move.

"I won't lie to you, Alain. You won't feel good for the next few hours. And probably worse afterward. Let me explain; you have ingurgitated an anesthetic drug cocktail mixed with your vodka. This drink was fixed by flight attendant Martine Laramée. You know her? No need to answer. She knows who you are. That's all that matters."

Alain Dupont's heart was pounding, and his mind felt like drifting away from his body, like he was watching this tragic comedy as a spectator. He didn't know of a Martine Laramée. He made a guttural sound trying to scream. It was the best he could do now. Michel Madison pursed his lips, feigning compassion.

"You see, now the other cocktail is kicking in. It's called Special K. Do you know what Special K is? It's the name given to ketamine. It's a powerful drug used mostly by veterinarians. But I assure you, they also use it on humans sometimes to treat extreme pain. You might rightly argue that one should not overuse the drug and that one should get another medicine to counteract the negative effects of the first, but then again, I'm not a doctor, so what do I know?"

Madison chuckled with a thunderous, evil laugh that sent chills down Dupont's spine. A force from behind grabbed him under the armpits and lifted him from his seat, long enough for a flight attendant to reach over and slide a blue padded blanket under him, and then he was dropped heavily. Madison was still watching him with amusement.

"One can never be too careful, can one, Alain? The next thing you know, you're pissing yourself. Because with the amount of Special K I've pumped into your arm, you might not be able to keep your bladder under control. We wouldn't want to ruin your seat fabric, now would we? You are probably wondering why I pumped a powerful painkiller into you when you are not suffering. Let's just say it's a preventive measure. I don't read tea leaves, Alain. But I have a feeling that in a few minutes, you will be glad that I injected you with this elixir."

Fear struck Alain Dupont greatly at the sight of Michel Madison's two arms, now completely covered with what looked like scales, like on the skin of a lizard. There were also some growing out of the base of his neck. Madison caught his distressed look and pouted disdainfully.

"I know. I have dry skin. What can I say? I forgot to bring my skin lotion."

Another cacophonic laugh, but this time everyone else was laughing out loud, too. Dupont realized that most of these people were staring at him with a strange look on their faces. Several passengers had stood up to watch the show. Dupont still didn't know what they expected to happen. Why were they all so interested in him? Why was he capti-vating them so much? People rarely gave a damn about him. He wasn't a celebrity. His life was painfully mundane, so why all the fuss?

"You know when I said that everyone hates you? That wasn't a pretense or a figure of speech. It was the honest truth. There's one caveat, though. I don't hate you. I didn't know you at all before tonight, so why should I hate you?

You have done nothing to me. So, if there's a solace in all this, just know that. But these guys? Oh boy, I mean, I don't know what you've done to them, but it must be huge because they hate your guts with a passion I've rarely seen in my lengthy life."

Alain Dupont braced himself when he saw Michel Madison lunge to hit him violently on his right shoulder. Strangely, he felt nothing.

"No feeling, eh?" Madison said, stunned. "This stuff is really powerful."

Madison grabbed a notebook and flipped through the handwritten pages, stopping at the spot he was looking for.

"Ketamine is such a powerful painkiller that people could get hurt and never know it. We've just proved it was the case. You confirm you didn't feel a thing?"

Unable to speak, Dupont looked at Madison, dismay in his eyes. He was concerned by his elevated heart rate, the only thing he could feel right now, as if his heart were a kite caught in a violent storm.

"It also seems that Special K can cause heart failures or strokes," Madison went on." Let's hope not, right?"

Michel Madison mockingly crossed his fingers.

"Let me ask you a question, Alain. Do you know why all these folks are here? And why do they hate you that much? Blink once if you do, twice if you don't."

Dupont blinked twice. Madison looked at him, perplexed as if he didn't believe him. He urged him to try, but Dupont batted his eyelids twice again.

"Denial is a powerful thing, isn't it, Claude?" Madison said, looking at an imposing man standing next to them.

This fellow Claude had been staring at Alain since the

beginning of this terrible act. He confirmed Madison's premise with a heavy and cavernous voice.

Madison put his hand on Dupont's arm, who still felt nothing, then came closer.

"You know what I think? I think you know. I think that deep down, you hope you're wrong, that it's not what you presume. Am I wrong?"

Dupont did not react. Madison's face hardened. He reiterated, raising his voice,

"Am I wrong?"

Dupont blinked twice. Madison's face relaxed.

"I thought so. The good news is that you know why they're here and why they hate you. But the bad news is that you know why they're here and why they hate you."

Dupont felt even more detached from his body as if he was flying over the scene yet facing Michel Madison at the same time. It was a peculiar sensation. Soothing and terrifying. Would he come down to normal eventually? Or would the drug that this psychopath had injected into his body kill him? Either way, it was too late. He was a bystander in this waking nightmare. He didn't understand the relationship between the past events and these people. Who were they? What was their relation to all this? What did they expect? An apology? A confession?

"Let me ask you another question, then. Do you still have nightmares? Do you still see the massive yellow mass? Do you still hear the screams?"

Alain felt he was losing his mind now. How did Madison know about the nightmares? About the screams? About the yellow mass? Who was he, and what kind of creature was he turning into, for fuck's sake? Then Dupont's heart skipped a beat as he looked at the remaining flight time on the screen: four hours and twenty-five minutes.

Shit, time was running backward.

Madison addressed the individuals standing nearby.

"Everything ready?"

"Yes," said someone in the back.

Madison looked at Dupont with an enthralling look. Then whispered something that scared the crap out of him.

"It's payback time, pal!"

Before he could react, Dupont felt he was being lifted and dragged to the back of the plane, pulled by two stocky men who were handling him like a sandbag. They carried him, then latched onto something, then let him fall back down. Except that there was something holding him up. As best he could, he raised his head to find out what was keeping him upright and saw chains screwed into the cabin, holding him up against his will. Dupont wanted to fight and kick, but his body still refused to obey. Then he saw the crowd glowering at him and Michel Madison approaching with jerky motions.

He had a huge smile that split half of his face from ear to ear with a bluffing amount of teeth in his mouth. His grin was wider than his face. It gave him a dislocated and evil face. His arms were covered with green and grey scales; his neck too. He walked with a hop, but like a zero gravity astronaut. And he was dancing, spinning in the air as if he wanted to make a spectacle of himself. He moved quickly toward Dupont and stopped a few inches from his face.

"You're probably wondering what we want from you, aren't you?"

Dupont's mind was wandering. He thought he was going crazy, as the scene was grotesque. How could Madison's grin distort his face so severely? How could he speak with his lips still? His face was frozen like it was carved from clay, giving only the grim vision of that damn demonic smile. Like the Joker in Batman, but stuck in wax.

Madison put his hand on Dupont's shoulder, and Alain screamed as he realized he was heading straight to hell.

13

———————

Dupont was screaming his lungs out. He gripped the steering wheel firmly in front of him. His knuckles were white as he gripped it tightly. The sun blinded him, and he immediately slammed on the brakes with all his might. The momentum threw him forward, but his seat belt held him in place. Thankfully, he regained control of his limbs and his body. He noticed his vehicle was veering slightly to the right, and for a moment, he feared that the truck would roll over onto its side. But the movement stopped, and he regained his senses.

Dupont squinted to look forward before even trying to figure out where he was and why he was no longer on the plane. He felt his hair straighten as he noticed the picture of Manon, his first girlfriend, embedded in a brown bead necklace hanging from his rearview mirror. There was only one place this necklace had been, only one place it could be right now: his former truck's cab. That was impossible since the truck had been destroyed decades ago. A voice on his right staggered him.

"You're wondering what we're doing here, aren't you?"

A vision of horror appeared. A fright that seized Dupont by the guts like an animal with sharp fangs. Michel Madison was sitting on the seat next to him, watching him through his enormous black eye sockets and still sporting that damn disjointed smile out of a freak nightmare.

Alain Dupont kept stoic, completely petrified. He felt like he was in a bad dream that wouldn't end. He knew he was still in that shitty plane, hanging by his wrists like Christ on the cross, ready to be crucified by a mob of idiots who claimed to know him. But he had no clue who they were. Why did they say they knew him? He looked through the windshield for the first time and saw a familiar sight that he had spent much of his life trying to forget. The one that still haunted his days and nights.

The yellow mass was there in the distance. In the same spot as always. The same place as in his most sadistic dreams. Except he didn't know if he was dreaming or if he was really there. It could only be a dream.

You couldn't relive the same experience twice, could you? No one could travel through time.

Something outside his cabin, diagonally to his right, caught his eye. Michel Madison was standing outside but no longer looked like himself. He looked more like a monster covered in evil armor glistening in the sun. He noticed Madison was talking to him but couldn't hear a word. His cabin was soundproofed. Then Madison appeared in the passenger seat again, out of nowhere. Dupont glanced outside where Madison had been a few seconds earlier; he was no longer there. He was relieved that this lunatic wasn't multiplying. Then Alain examined Madison's face for the first time. It was becoming more and more distorted as time passed. Panic gripped him by the throat.

"What the fuck are you?" Alain asked, shouting.

Madison shrieked a hollow laugh and looked at him with an entertained face.

"You want to talk about that now?"

"Yes, I do."

"Okay, but I would get out of here as fast as humanly possible if I were you."

Dupont had time to see a flame lick his right cheek before he jumped out of the vehicle by opening the door on his left. He groaned as he fell heavily onto the pavement. He painfully got up and staggered away from the burning truck. Alain caught up with the frightening figure that Michel Madison had become, then looked back to see the enormous truck burning at a breakneck speed.

"What does this all mean?" Alain asked in a tormented voice.

"That you were wise to get out of that truck!"

Madison snapped his slender fingers adorned with long claws, and something violently hurled Dupont backward, blown by the powerful blast of the van that had disintegrated a few dozen meters away. Alain rubbed his head to get rid of the pain and carefully stood up. All his limbs were hurting.

"Why am I here? Why do I have to go through this again?"

Michel Madison shrugged, still showing his disproportionate smile.

"Tell me, goddammit. Who are you? What have you turned into? Are you a monster or something?"

Madison rolled his huge, dark eyes.

"A monster. Big words right away."

"You're the antichrist, then?"

Madison seemed surprised by the suggestion and nodded slightly.

"If you will, I'm what they call a fixer."

"A fixer?"

"Precisely."

Dupont pondered for a few seconds, still not figuring out what this had to do with him. Hadn't he already paid his dues dearly? Madison waved him off to let him know it didn't matter. Dupont was alarmed when he heard the blood-curdling wailing coming from behind.

"Ha, the screams," Michel Madison said, sounding much too cheerful.

Dupont didn't dare turn to face them; he knew too well where this was coming from. It wasn't the first time he had been standing there or experienced this situation or heard those nagging screams. Now it was just a nightmare that his sick mind had fabricated. The more he wanted to run away from this terrible memory, the more it came crashing back to hurt him again and again. To remind him how much he had to make amends. He had spent most of his adult life trying to forget, and he had been reliving these terrible things day after day, night after night. But not like this. Not to this extent. Not that real. Not that cruel.

"Look."

"No."

Madison's voice rose and sounded otherworldly.

"I said look."

It wasn't an option. Alain Dupont shivered with fear. He had never been so scared in his life. Not even when it happened the first time, but this time, it was horrifying and gripping him by its very core. He turned to the screams and immediately recognized them, just like in his memory. Still unbearable.

"I can't."

"Go on," Madison yelled.

"No, I can't."

"NOW!"

Dupont had fled in the opposite direction. It surprised him that Madison didn't stop him. Would he really simply let him get away? Could it be that easy?

And just like that, a force lifted Alain off the ground and threw him backward. As if he was tied to a strong rubber band, pulling him back to the same location every time he tried to take off.

He heard even more intense screams but realized they were his own. He was now trapped in the ravine, in that foul pool, surrounded by screams of pain and deadly silence. And right in front of him, staring at him with a dejected look, stood his own motionless figure. He felt he was suffocating, drowning with all those hands pulling him down the ravine. The further down he went, the more he lost contact with his body image on the road and the less he could breathe. Then he screamed,

"I'm suffocating. Help me. I'm drowning."

But his body double was observing him helplessly. He simply stared at him alongside Michel Madison, who had danced again with sinister steps, spinning around and laughing out loud.

Dupont knew that there was only one thing left to do.

Dying.

14

———

His back turned to Alain Dupont, Michel Madison seemed to speak to a crowd as his previously unintelligible words became clearer. No doubt Dupont was back on the plane, and that suited him fine. He would rather be there than relive the fear he felt a few seconds earlier in the ravine. It was overwhelming. Here, at least, he still had a slim chance of making it out alive.

Looking up, he noticed his wrists were still attached to the ceiling of the aircraft. He also realized that his shoulders had dislocated because of the weight of his body pulling him to the ground, but he still felt no pain. Madison's terrifying face turned to him, and realizing that Alain had regained consciousness, he broke out into his evil grin, his sharp, vile teeth, and turned in the opposite direction.

"Ladies and gentlemen, let me remind you of the rules. You have two strokes. I respect your rage but leave some for the rest of us. And for God's sake, don't go for the head. We want him fully aware. We want him to listen."

He ended his sentence with a roar of laughter, causing

the others to chuckle as well. Alain Dupont tilted his head to the side to see more clearly, but Michel Madison's enormous carcass was in the way. It was only then that it hit him hard. How much bigger and taller Madison was than before! Hell, he must have been close to seven feet tall by now and probably added about fifty pounds of muscle to his frame. And Dupont also realized at this point that the monster was naked. Scales were covering his entire body, and his eyes were completely black. He looked like a creepy lizard. Gone was the glowing costume of his nightmare. This son of a bitch was morphing at lightning speed.

Dupont was struck with a huge fear when Madison moved to the side to display a horrifying vision: all the passengers were waiting in line, watching him with a sinister look, and he saw the man at the beginning of the line, the man from the airport who had confronted him in the bathroom. He grabbed an aluminum baseball bat with a grotesque, evil-looking clown face painted on it. He walked up to Dupont and, red-faced, said horrible things to him.

"My father killed himself two years later, you piece of shit."

He lunged backward and slammed the baseball bat into Dupont's ribs, and once again, he felt nothing except for the recoil from the impact. He couldn't speak. He could only look at his assailant begging for mercy. He didn't know who this guy was, just like he didn't for those waiting in line. But they seemed to know him and, worse, wanted him harmed. What the hell did he do to them, for crying out loud?

The imposing man enjoyed the moment for an instant that lasted forever. Then he swung again, this time across Alain's left knee, dislocating the joint, so his leg twirled in front of his face before dropping to the ground. The foot pointed completely backward. Dupont did not understand why he did not feel any pain. Of course, Madison had given him Special K or whatever the shit was called, but people were amputating his body with a baseball bat. How was that possible? What did that mean, and more importantly, what the fuck was going on?

Madison howled with laughter at Dupont's dislocated leg and congratulated the man on his major league hit. The monster was still twirling around. He had one arm in front of him, the other above his head like a flamenco dancer. The imposing figure handed over his bat to a woman who was staring at Dupont with soul-crushing sadism in her eyes.

"You motherfucker. Do you know all the things I could have done if I had not crossed your path, scumbag?"

She launched from the ground up and slammed the bat between Dupont's legs. Madison bellowed with pleasure.

"In the balls," he laughed loudly, almost hysterically. "Straight into the nuts."

And he laughed like a madman. And the others were also laughing, being so excited by what was happening out there.

For her second stroke, the woman swung the bat down on Dupont's shoulder, lightly clipping his ear and tearing off half of it. Content, she handed the bat to the next man in line, a tall, lanky guy. He looked at Dupont playfully.

"You know what's funny? I was the best baseball player in my town before all this. So, I figure this is a fortunate turn of events. Don't you think, asshole?"

Not waiting for an answer, he struck Dupont violently in the ribs, only to fear that Dupont's rib cage became distorted from the impact. The man realized that he broke his left ribs and worried they would puncture his heart. He turned to

Madison fearfully, but the creature motioned him to go on, saying that everything was fine. The man didn't want to take the fun out of it by killing him. He hit him more carefully on the right elbow this time, knocking Dupont's arm back. Dupont's eyes widened as his limb popped out outward, pointing at a forty-five-degree angle. He felt despair sweep over him, but he couldn't cry. After the second blow, the man had turned to the crowd, triumphant, his arms in the air.

"Didn't I mention that I'm a baseball all-star? Look how I beat the crap out of him."

He contemplated his masterpiece one last time, smiling, then handed the bat to someone else.

Dupont nearly passed out several times, but Madison snapped him back to reality by poking his arm with his scratched and chipped hand.

"No, not yet. Stay with us."

And Dupont regained his senses as if someone had just injected him with a powerful dose of adrenaline. He had to put up with the insults and abuse of all these people, watch his body break apart, watch his testicles being crushed, especially by women, and realize that his limbs were no longer anything like they used to be.

He suffered several open fractures, visible bones protruding from his body like long, sharp thorns from a rosebush. The remaining people were having fun hitting the prominent bones with the baseball bat. No one had any shame or restraint; they beat him relentlessly and with abandon; even the female flight attendants obviously had something against him. The only person not taking part in this slaughter was Michel Madison. He was leading the charge like a master of ceremonies from hell. Satan himself could not have been more barbaric, more ruthless.

All these people were about the same age, about thirty years old. They all had their faces twisted with hatred, foaming at the mouth like dogs drooling with rage. They all hit him shamelessly. The clown painted on the baseball bat came down on him with fury, his evil face staring into his eyes with delight. Like he was alive.

Dupont checked his legs and noticed that one of them was only held by shreds of flesh, the other totally dislocated. The same thing for his arms still raised above his head and held his carcass with increasing difficulty. There were several open fractures, so much so that Dupont wondered how they could still hold his body upright. In addition, Alain could hardly breathe, probably because of his punctured lungs caused by his sunken ribs.

He stared at Madison, who was looking back at him with an outrageous smile and inky eyes. He no longer danced, merely stared at him with a mixture of amusement and disdain. Those who had already hit him returned to the front of the plane to drink champagne. Only two people left had still not quenched their bloodthirsty rage. There was not much left to smash, anyway. All that remained was his head, which was intact. But only because Madison had warned them not to target it.

They followed his instructions to the T. Dupont was stunned that this monster had such a grip on them despite their apparent anger. He was surprised that no one disobeyed and shattered his brain. And why weren't they appalled by the monster Madison had become? Perhaps they saw him in his human shape? Maybe to them, Madison was still that slender, distinguished guy with azure eyes? Maybe only Dupont saw the true nature of the beast. The sole person to see how evil he was.

Alain spotted a guy in the background who looked familiar. The man was simply observing him quietly. He had not been part of the carnage, at least not that he could remember. But why did his face look so familiar? Why did he stay away? Then he recognized him, clear as day. The brown jacket and the black tie. It was the little boy with the dinosaurs from earlier—the kid with the bloody mouth. He figured out who he was when he saw him in his adult form. He looked down. He could still see his big, frightened eyes and his open mouth—the look on his face, terrified in death.

Dupont was on the verge of passing out when Madison approached, his huge face inches from his ear.

"You know what the worst part is? You think you've been through hell and back with all these people hating you so much. They hit you with all their might with a baseball bat. You figure that nothing worse could possibly happen. But I promise you. It pales in comparison to when the drug stops working, and your body will wake up from its slumber."

Dupont wanted to scream, but he was still mute. He looked at the demon with terror. Madison laughed as he danced around. He was spinning like a top going up and down in the air inside the cockpit. He was laughing his ass off. Everyone had looked back at Alain and was laughing as hard as Madison.

Then the monster whirled around him again, grabbed him by the throat, and ripped him from his bonds. Then, in a cheerful voice, he said,

"Jesus Christ, buddy, look at you. You need to get some fresh air."

With a sharp gesture, he threw Dupont toward the portholes on his left, but instead of crashing against the wall as he should have, he went through the tiles and suddenly found himself thirty-five thousand feet in the air. He shouted, and this time his voice was audible. His body was descending in free flight at an alarming rate, so much so that he wondered how it was possible for him to breathe at that altitude. Why wasn't he fainting?

Then he saw the earth approaching at breakneck speed.

He screamed one last time as he closed his eyes.

15

Alain Dupont felt numb and disoriented. Strong sun rays had blinded him, and the photo of his ex was hanging on his right side in a wooden necklace. He was sitting down and held securely by his seatbelt, watching the road slip away under him, his eyes unable to see properly.

He hadn't felt like this for a long time, nor had he felt the salutary effects of alcohol. He smiled as his arms were back to their normal state, and his legs were functioning and, most importantly, at the right angle. But the reality came crashing in as he realized that the plane, all those people striking him, the hideous and ghastly Michel Madison, was nothing compared to the nightmare he had just come through and nothing compared to the next thing to come.

He wouldn't wake up in his bed drenched in sweat this time. There was no way out! This time it was it. He was a captive of this traumatic and evil fantasy, like a prisoner on an incomplete roller coaster. Dupont raised his two weighty arms and clumsily reached for the enormous steering wheel. His eyes squinted to see clearly. Maybe this was his redeeming chance? Maybe he could change things? Change the past? Maybe this was what these people expected from him.

Dupont thrust both feet on the brake, but he still missed the target. He bent down to look for the pedal on the floor, and, dammit, there was none. He was helpless. He knew it was imminent. He had just passed the small red-roofed farmhouse and was approaching the stop sign he wouldn't make. His eyelids grew heavy as if he was falling asleep. He yelled to stay awake and tried to roll down the window on his left, but the handle snapped in his hand after half a turn. Everything in this truck prevented him from accomplishing what he was supposed to do. He would be a passive witness to the horrific scene about to happen, once again, twenty years later, almost to the day.

His eyes filled with tears as he watched the huge yellow vehicle approaching to his right, unsuspecting of the catastrophe ahead. Dupont kicked the floorboard beneath with such force that his foot broke through the truck's carpet and got stuck. Dupont stared at the oncoming vehicle. The path was clear since Dupont was supposed to stop. He shouted, "Brake! Brake, goddamn it!" to the driver. But like the first time, the other vehicle didn't stop. Like the first time, he relied on an alcohol-induced Alain Dupont to do what he was supposed to do. Alain Dupont thought it was no big deal to drink that much, that he wasn't that drunk coming from his lunch with a friend. He had dozed off at the wheel, only to wake up when the other driver blew his horn, just long enough to see that neither he nor the other guy had enough time to slam on the brakes, that there was no way to avoid the crash. Dupont, in his massive steel monster, his tank full of fuel, was arriving like a missile with its eighteen tons accentuated by its momentum.

Dupont once again saw the driver's terror-distorted face before the impact. They had looked each other in the eyes, knowing what was coming like inseparable partners in this deadly outcome. Then there was a moment of utter peace as if everything was floating away, silently—the last hope before the brutal collision.

And that noise.

That infernal noise of twisting metal and a deafening explosion was like a huge rocket striking a colossal target. If someone had wanted to coordinate the accident to create this perfect storm on purpose, he would never have been able to do it. Once again, Dupont lost track of his surroundings amidst the terrifying crash of the truck's front end and its cargo violently veering to the right. The load had failed to resist the ten-wheeler force of inertia, which had decelerated almost completely in a matter of seconds, propelling the driver forward, well secured by his seatbelt, which he had fastened for a rare occasion.

As though, instinctively, he knew what was coming. He knew his selfishness had pushed him to drink even though he was smart enough to realize it was too much. The same selfishness made him drive that oil-filled bomb capable of destroying almost everything in its path. And it was at that moment he concluded that not caring about others' faith wasn't a reason to cause his own demise. He had buckled up, just in case.

In retrospect, he would rather have died. Sometimes death is sweeter than survival.

He once again watched in terror as the bus was tossed into the air, spinning several times before shattering into pieces to the ground. He once again saw the tiny bodies being thrown out of the vehicle, shredded, like little angels flying up into the sky. Except that he knew it was the other way around. They weren't going to heaven. They were crashing down on the road like rag dolls in the awful impact of a mass hitting the ground. He only hoped they were already dead when they smashed to the ground, for the image of their tiny skeletons on the asphalt was unbearable.

Several minutes had passed before Alain Dupont realized what had just happened. He remembered the smell of oil coming from the back of the truck, mixed with the smell of rubber and powder from the brakes. He recalled the yellow school bus, ripped apart like the Titanic, half lying in the ravine to his right, and the rest in the middle of the road. He thought of the bodies near the school bus, mutilated, torn from their limbs and sometimes even from their heads. He remembered that a force had driven him to get out of his cabin. It told him he had to get away from his truck at all costs.

Except that getting away meant getting closer to infamy. Who could live a normal life, having seen all these disarticulated child bodies on the road and in the ravine? Who could live a normal life being responsible for such havoc? That it was all his fault. He had fallen asleep, overly intoxicated by the booze he had consumed half an hour earlier.

Nobody was around. No cars, no witnesses. Only Dupont and the children. As if people were thoughtful enough to save this moment for them. As if they had to live this in privacy. Dupont moved forward, making a concerted effort not to look at the corpses lying at his feet.

Then, a gigantic explosion had thrown him forward, and he had crashed to the ground, face down as if somebody had pushed him from behind. Was it Michel Madison who had stood there the whole time? Even when it happened? Was Michel Madison the monster who had caused all this? The evil mastermind who had taken control of him and made him drink more than he should have? Who had orchestrated the cohesive impact.

He turned to check if he was back there, but he wasn't. Alain was alone with the victims, as he had been back then. He looked forward and had the impulse to backtrack at the sight of a child's crippled body with brown hair and eyes like sepia marbles. He had a grimace like an evil grin, his jaw broken. Another small boy lay dead ahead, staring at him with blank eyes. He wore a T-shirt with a decal of a plane flying into a storm.

Dupont stood up and walked away, even though he knew he was doing the wrong thing, that he was only looking out for himself. He got closer to the yellow bus that still had its mandatory stop lights on as if the driver had intended to protect the kids before the impact. Dupont could have sworn that the blinkers weren't on when the crash occurred, but maybe he was wrong. It happened so fast.

He stepped over the dead bodies, consciously ignoring them. He noticed the driver was still trapped in his seat, restrained by his seatbelt, a luxury the children hadn't had, except that it hadn't been enough to save his life. You don't get out unscathed from a shock of such magnitude, a gliding lift in the air, or a fatal whirlwind. Dupont approached the driver's window with hushed steps, and what he discovered made his blood run cold. He clamped his hand over his mouth as he watched the driver with his head resting on the steering wheel. His face was toward Dupont as if he were scrutinizing him, along with the same frightened expression on his face as the first time. His eyes were wide open as if he were asking for help. His mouth fully stretched as if he were screaming in terror as he died. His forehead cracked in two like a coconut split with a machete. Dupont could see the gray matter of his brain leaking from his skull.

He had recognized him. It was him, the boy in the suit and tie. It was him, the kid who played with dinosaurs, who had smiled with a bloody mouth. It was him, the man in the background, who watched him while the others shamelessly beat him. Dupont didn't know what he had done to deserve his mercy, but he was grateful. And that was when he had first heard the screams, the horrible, mournful howls coming from the ravine!

What he did next would change the course of his life forever.

And cause his downfall.

16

———————

"What the hell is this?" Alain Dupont thought as he walked toward the ditch, even though he already knew the answer. It was his lame way of hoping for a different turn of events, that it wouldn't be what he feared. A smell of sulfur wafted from the school bus, but Dupont later realized it was the smell of burning blood. Concentration camp survivors said that what remained from their time in those horrible places was the atmosphere of death that prevailed, the smell of people burning. Alain Dupont was far from being one of them. To be honest, he had more in common with their tormentors than with the survivors. Unfortunately, that was what had also stuck with him from that horrific accident— the atmosphere of death and the smell of burning blood.

Then he stopped dead in his tracks when he first saw what he had feared. Children's severed corpses, some with their heads ripped off, looking absent with their eyes half closed. Where did the laments come from if this ravine had turned into a mass grave? Dupont didn't dare to move closer. Fear was grabbing him by his guts, like when you can't step over the edge of a precipice for fear of plunging into it. Then, he saw the first imploring eyes and understood where the crying was coming from. Small fighting souls, still alive, tenaciously refusing to surrender.

They saw their savior in Alain Dupont, the one through whom they could get out of this muddy tomb alive. The man watched them from afar in silence. His eyes were expressive, showing how much he wished that they had ended up with someone else, someone more courageous, someone better than him. Dupont's eyes begged for mercy and forgiveness.

The kids knew they were doomed as he backed away from them. They shouted even louder, seeming to sway him to do something one last time. That awful roar that had haunted his nights since his cowardice was so vile that he could no longer live with himself. He had a second chance to do the right thing, but he was about to screw up again. To let himself down, and worse, to leave these kids to their fate.

It suddenly came to him like an impulse. He realized that there was no way out if he stayed put. Rescuing the kids meant that he would have to stay until help arrived. Many were already dead. The images of all those little cherubs dismembered and crushed would be visible to others, and no one would be immune to the horrific sight. Faced with the bruised, torn, and battered children's body parts.

If he stayed, no one would care about his good deed, about saving a few kids. They would treat him like a monster, anyway. He'd had a lot more to drink than he should have. His breath reeked of alcohol. His clouded brain hadn't noticed the mandatory stop sign at the intersection. The sun in his face hadn't helped either, but there was no excuse for launching several tons of steel at a school bus full of infants starting out on their life journey.

Nothing he could say would make up for any of it. He would turn into an outcast. Even if he ever got out of prison, his life was over. The roadblocks to his future were right there, deep in the mud of that ravine in which the small, damaged carcasses lay. He didn't know why then, and he still doesn't know why now, but he thought his only chance to save himself was to flee.

He would have time to sober up before they found him. At worst, once he came to his senses, he could turn himself in and say that he had panicked at the sight of all those frail bodies strewn across the road and grass; he could say that none of them were alive, a lie he would take to his grave.

He wished that the truck explosion had erased all traces of his presence. He wished the blaze would hinder the work of the police and that it would be a while before they could piece together what had happened.

Of course, he was in tremendous pain all over, so he ran out through the cornfields as far as the eye could see and ran for what seemed like an eternity. He never looked back and only stopped when the screams had faded away because he was so far away that he couldn't hear them anymore or simply because fate had done its work.

He had then reached a road, then a small stream. He laid down in the grass by the water's edge after splashing the icy water on his body to erase all traces of his mishap. There was no more dust on his clothes or sulfur on the fabric. Only scratches on his hands and forearms resulted from glass fragments that had shattered on him.

He watched the sky, hoping for some answer that wouldn't come. He could replay over and over everything that had happened in his head, and nothing justified what he had just done. No one could come out unscathed from escaping instead of saving children's lives. It was a decision that would drive any normal person crazy. The human brain could endure some degree of insanity, but at some point, it became unmanageable.

That probably what was happening since he had set foot in the airport: he was crazy. That's why he envisioned Michel Madison morphing into a gruesome monster. That's why he didn't feel a thing when all those half-crazed passengers beat him furiously. That's why he was constantly wavering from one world to another. From the plane to the accident, back to the plane, and still behind his truck wheel again.

It was the only logical explanation, but there was one thing that troubled him. If he really was delusional, if he really was imagining things, then why was he conscious? After all, when we sleep, we don't show up in the middle of our dream and say, "I know, I'm dreaming." So how could it differ from madness? Was there a portion of our mind that remained lucid on the sideline? While the reptilian brain dived into delusion, the limbic brain gained perspective. Or was it the other way around?

The other option was even more terrifying. What if it were true? What if he wasn't delirious? What if he was really going through this? The smell of blood was so authentic. Dupont knew exactly what would happen from there. He would go home. A few hours later, six police cars would show up at his apartment, and once again, his first instinct would be to run away. But unsuccessfully this time. The rest; jail, family and public disgrace, and his difficult social reinsertion once he was released for good behavior. But above all, the memory and the nightmares of those screams, the dismembered bodies, the driver's face frozen in horror forever. He could not go through this once more.

Then there were these. The plane, Madison, the beatings. Like a sentence that Dupont foresaw. After all, didn't we all live by the moral compass our parents taught us? If we did something wrong, would we pay the price a hundredfold? What was worse than killing children? What was worse than declining to help, to let them die? What could be worse than choosing oneself at the expense of a few children's lives? Nothing could justify it. So surely what was happening was fair. And if so, why was Dupont so scared? Why was he not prepared to accept it with serenity? Or was his fear part of his punishment? They say that to win without risk is a triumph without glory. Perhaps it was the same in the expiation of his sins?

He felt a force grabbing him so tightly that his entire frame contorted, and he was in so much pain that his eyes revulsed. Yet he didn't lose conscience. He was in more pain than the human brain could normally go through. He immediately knew why amid his dizzying screams and unbearable pain when he saw Michel Madison leaning over him, one hand on his body and his crazy, unbridled, delirious smile on his face.

Dupont was back in the plane, crushed to the ground, right in the middle of the aisle, and he was screaming to the point where his eardrums were in danger of cracking at any moment. And the more he screamed, the more Madison laughed, the more his enormous mouth widened as if he was going to swallow Alain in one fell swoop, and his eyes grew wider. The foul scent coming from the monster's throat had made its way into Dupont's nostrils, and he thought he was about to puke,until he realized it was exactly the same as in the ravine, the smell of burning blood. But he could no longer hear the screams, only his own.

He gasped as he saw what looked like little hands clawing at Madison's throat, like children grabbing grass and mud in the ravine in a last-ditch effort to get to the surface. Then Madison stood up, and Dupont noticed the crowd in front and finally realized what was happening. He understood that the adults in the plane, the ones that Michel Madison handled like a grand maestro, the ones who were beating him with such fury and abandon were, in fact, the children he had killed that day, at the age they would be today. The children he left for dead in the ditch.

Instead of the adults from before, there was now a procession of kids staring at him. Kids with peach skin and pink cheekbones who looked at him, their faces completely stoic. Dupont recognized some of them. These faces had never faded from his memory. He was condemned to be reminded of them as long as he lived, and maybe even after, who knows?

Dupont felt dizzy when he realized that his right arm was no longer tied to his body. He looked up at the ceiling of the plane and saw his arm hanging down, still clinging to the tie that had held him upright earlier. He looked at his other arm, which was still hanging to his left shoulder, but only by a few shreds of flesh and ligaments.

His legs were so mangled that they pointed in opposite directions, in a no longer human shape. He looked like a disarticulated dummy dropped on the floor at the end of a performance. He could no longer move except for his head.

The children moved toward him, looking impassive. The footsteps sounded heavy, like soldiers on parade. The cadence was perfect, and Madison marveled at them like a sculptor proud of his work. Then he looked at Dupont crushed to the ground with his big, black, mischievous eyes.

His huge, inflated smile had not faded from his face since the beginning. This thing was fulfilling its destiny.

It was the highlight of the show, his purpose in life. The reason he was on this flight was to fulfill his larger-than-life calling. He had referred to it. He was the fixer. What he was searching for the children was reparation. And they would get it, whether or not Dupont wanted it. The justice of men had failed these kids, but the justice of the fixer would not. Not with an overexcited Michel Madison watching the show's finale like a spectator on the edge of his seat, ecstatic at the crescendo he was expecting from one moment to the next, chills all over his scaly body.

The first children carved a grin on their fragile little faces, and their eyes became stern. Then their smile also widened beyond what was humanly imaginable. Their tiny baby teeth gave way to sharp yellowed teeth. Their skin turned green as they moved forward, and they all turned into short, scaly-skinned gargoyles. Those who followed experienced the same grotesque metamorphosis as they approached, as if in a macabre dance set to perfection.

Alain Dupont felt the pain lessen as the adrenaline flooded in what remained of his connected nerves. He was so frightened that his mouth was wide open as if he was screaming, but he could no longer make any sound. He realized his face looked exactly the same as the bus driver's—that catatonic look of death. Like an inescapable accident, like when a tanker full of fuel was about to annihilate you, and you only had time to make eye contact with the driver who had already given up trying to save your life.

The small demons had approached Alain Dupont's lying carcass with an intimidating demeanor, now cackling like a horde of hyenas surrounding a wounded prey, their frightening eyes showing that they would soon feast on his flesh and entrails. The laughter of the creatures intensified as others gathered above those on the bottom, building a pyramid, an insurmountable wall. Alain Dupont was doomed but not stunned. What puzzled him was how long it took. He thought he would have paid the price for his cowardice long ago.

Then, just as the gargoyles perched higher up, backing off a bit to rush toward him, Alain Dupont was no longer afraid. Instead, he was filled with a blissful and quite surprising realization, given the circumstances and the teeth that were now grabbing him by the throat, shaking him powerfully so that pieces of flesh would give way to their bite, about to tear everything off in their wake.

The last thought of Alain Dupont's existence was an indisputable assessment, as frightening as it was soothing. As clear as it was grim.

He deserved to die.

17

———

Myriam Gagnon had hung up the phone when a colleague, with whom she had planned to have dinner this evening, asked her if she had heard from her boyfriend. She realized that he should have called her by now to advise her of his arrival. He should have landed half an hour ago and had sworn to call her as soon as his plane touched the runway. She asked for another drink, as she would obviously still be waiting. Perhaps his flight had been delayed a tad. She didn't know which website to search for flight tracking. A colleague had told her once, but she hadn't written it down.

The waiter smiled warmly at her as he slid a glass of vodka cranberry her way. She took a sip and winced. She sighed as she looked at her watch for the third time in a few minutes. A man walked up and tried to strike up a conversation, but she had no interest in talking, let alone being charmed by anyone.

She only hoped that her fears were unfounded. She wished she was wrong, thinking that Alain could not get on the plane, that he had chickened out as he boarded. If he did, then she knew what it meant, and it made her feel profoundly sad and depressed. Luckily, they weren't living together. It would make things a lot easier should they break up.

She shook her head—no time to ponder such dark thoughts. A lot could have warranted his silence. Maybe his cell phone was dead, maybe the plane was delayed, maybe he had forgotten to call her in the heat of the moment. Surely there was a logical explanation.

The man next to her was still staring at her with a goofy smile, so much so that she sighed impatiently.

"I don't want to bother you, believe me," he said.

He was tall and lanky, with a nice demeanor. His voice was soft and soothing. Myriam looked at him and smiled. He had done nothing to her, after all. There was no need to make life difficult for him. And who knows, maybe a chat would help ease the tension until she figured out Alain's deal.

"Sorry, I'm just a little worried, that's all."

The man raised his glass and smiled warmly.

Myriam flinched as she felt her cell phone vibrate, but it was Clara, another of her friends, checking in. She was about to ask her to stop calling and to tell the others until she got in touch with her boyfriend, but she refrained. She didn't have to afflict those who were worried about her with her bad mood. It wasn't their fault she had no sign of Alain, either. Myriam talked with Clara for a few minutes, suggesting she go to the restaurant without her, that she would meet them as soon as she knew what happened to her boyfriend.

She resisted from mentioning the other option, giving up on her couple and meeting them by herself, making up a last-minute excuse. She scrutinized the man sitting a few benches to her right watching the television tennis match while sipping his drink. He was in his mid-fifties and well-groomed. He seemed well off financially, and that appealed to her. Basically, he was the kind of man that would normally attract her, even though he was the opposite of what Alain was. He was also the type of guy that had hurt her so much in the past. He was the sort she wanted to distance herself from.

She stared again at her mobile device screen and sighed.

"He won't come."

Myriam turned to the stranger, who kept watching the game as if nothing had happened.

"I beg your pardon?"

He finished his drink and looked at her sorrowfully.

"I said the man you're waiting for won't show up."

She felt anger grip her throat. How dare he say such a thing knowing absolutely nothing about her, and especially nothing about Alain? She was obviously worried. Why was he using it against her? Then her frustration gave way to perplexity. How did he know she was waiting for someone who wasn't already here? After all, she could sigh because of a friend, a relative staying at this hotel, or even a spouse who had stumbled across a baccarat table. The man stood up and grabbed his raincoat from the back of his seat.

"How would you know?" she said after a few seconds, her voice trembling with a mixture of rage and concern.

He looked at her with his gentle eyes, then smiled.

"Suffice to say; I have a gift."

He nodded and walked away in the opposite direction. Myriam Gagnon just stood there, stunned at the scene. She would tell Alain and her colleagues about this encounter. It would be a very interesting anecdote. But as she finished her drink, she couldn't help but feel that the man was probably right. That Alain wasn't coming! That it was over between them!

She wondered if he had at least bothered to go to the airport, and that was when he had quit. Or even worse, he had never left his house and hadn't even made an effort. She resented him for not at least calling to tell her. Even a text message, though a weak response, would have been preferable to the anguish of silence.

She dialed Alain's cell phone number but got a notice from her cell phone provider it was impossible to perform this action. Yet, she was receiving calls from her colleagues and friends with no problem. She did a test and contacted her office, and hung up when she heard the welcome message from the phone system.

Had he also canceled his phone? Had he taken his treachery that far? She knew she could frighten men, but this much? To the point of making them so soft? Then she calmed down by assuming that if he had deactivated his line, the system would say that the number was no longer in service, not that it was impossible to perform the requested operation.

She spotted a display board in the distance, behind the slot machines. It looked like a monitor, like those found in airports listing arrivals and departures, as well as boarding gates.

She slid twenty dollars on the counter, grabbed her purse and coat, and quickly got up to head to the monitor. She felt her heart pound as she realized that this was indeed the Las Vegas airport flight log. She recalled Alain's flight number, AC810, and scrolled through each line, standing in the middle of the passageway in front of the huge blue screen. She started at the top and read line by line.

She was getting to the flights from Montreal when she was jolted. An icy hand rested on her shoulder, making her take her eyes off the monitor for a few seconds. She turned and saw the man from the bar walking away, still holding his raincoat under his arm. Then she felt a gigantic hot wave, like a heat stroke, through her body. She stiffened, then loosened up.

It was as if time had stopped. She looked around, trying to figure out what she was doing there, standing in the middle of the hallway in front of a big blue screen. It was as if she had lost track of reality for a moment. How could she have walked to this place and not remember why she had gone there? Like when you walk to a room with a specific purpose and don't recall what you wanted to do once you get there, distracted by something else along the way.

She laughed and moved toward the hotel entrance to get her thoughts in order. What did she need to do again? Oh yes, dinner with her co-workers. There were a few of them extending their stay. Some had brought their spouses along, while others, like Myriam, were traveling solo. You never know what might happen in the City of Vice. After all, didn't they say what happens in Vegas stays in Vegas? Reaching the hotel's lobby, she ran into her good friend Clara, who ran up to her and kissed her on the cheeks.

"Conference is over, Myriam. Time to party, to have fun. There will surely be hot guys tonight. Come on. We'll be late for the restaurant. Everyone is waiting for us."

Myriam Gagnon smiled and followed her lead for what was to be an eventful evening.

18

———————

Claude Bouchard had been on the phone for more than an hour in the Maple Leaf VIP lounge, to the dismay of customers who were sighing with frustration. No one dared ask him to lower his voice, hoping that one of the lounge employees would come to their rescue. The imposing, middle-aged man with a receding hairline and harsh eyes was yelling at someone on the other end of the line.

A man with a sympathetic face was reading a paper on the other end and absentmindedly watching him with a smile. He understood the aggravation of people around Bouchard, many of whom had picked up their things and moved further away. It was shocking how Claude Bouchard had no regard for others. No matter who he disturbed, he would do what he pleased and screw community living.

The man with the newspaper went over to Bouchard and sat directly ahead in the chair. The latter gave him a harsh look, not too keen on having someone invade his space. But the other guy didn't mind greeting him with a nod that wasn't reciprocated.

The man looked around at his surroundings and smiled at the patrons nearby, and most of them smiled back at him. Surely they wished he had the guts to stand up to the guy on the phone and restore peace to the place.

The man leaned toward Bouchard.

"I'm getting a beer. Can I get you anything?"

Claude Bouchard glared at him blankly. The man asked again. Bouchard lowered his phone just long enough to reply in a deep voice,

"You clearly can see that I'm on the phone, you idiot. Get lost!"

The man didn't lose his cool, still leaning forward as if waiting for an answer. Bouchard sighed and waved him off.

"I'll take that as a no," the man said, laughing, and stood up.

Claude Bouchard told the man he would call him back later, and he had to have some good news. He would be at his Palm Beach condo in a few hours, which would give him plenty of time to correct what Bouchard was blaming him for. The latter hung up and put his phone down on the table in front, much to the guests' relief.

Bouchard didn't care. He had built his wealth by doing as he pleased, not caring about stepping on anyone's toes. He thought you couldn't make an omelet without breaking eggs. And God knows he had broken some eggs. And he still did when necessary. But because he was a wealthy man and owned a large portfolio of rental properties around the world, he now relied on his associates to do the dirty work. He hired people like him to support the business. Shameless, hard-nosed people for whom the goal of every negotiation was to get the most out of his rival. To hell with win-win deals. That was a concept for losers.

Bouchard watched the easy-going gentleman who had sat next to him a few minutes earlier as if captivated. He didn't intimidate the man, unlike he did with most people. No one in a normal mental state would have thought it was wise to bother him while he was on the phone. Yet he had done it. He must be some kind of freak who wasn't aware of the danger around.

Claude Bouchard was staring at the man as he chatted with folks around the buffet. These individuals seemed captivated by the man with the engaging look of a ministry professor. He was quite tall, Bouchard guessed about six feet, but slim. An androgynous body like that of a ballet dancer. He scrutinized his every move, fascinated by this unusual fellow, notwithstanding his insignificant appearance.

Then the man came back to his seat, holding a plate of food in one hand and two Heinekens in the other. He smiled at Bouchard and left one of the two beers on the table between them.

"I thought you might be thirsty after talking on the phone all that time. Your throat must be dry."

Claude Bouchard was suspicious by nature. He assumed everyone was a crook until proven otherwise. But he had to work hard to keep his judgment in check with this man he fancied. Bouchard was used to dealing with people he intimidated, so he didn't know how to react to the youthful carelessness of this guy who didn't seem to know who he was or how much fear he could inflict on others if they didn't do what he asked.

For the first time, Bouchard smiled, grabbed the collar of his Heineken bottle, and brought it up to his mouth, not taking his eyes off the man. Then he settled back into his seat, still staring at him with a bemused grin. The man smiled back at him, not at all disconcerted to be scrutinized by his imposing counterpart.

"You're a peculiar guy, aren't you?"

The man didn't know what to reply to his vague question. He simply shrugged and pursed his lips. When he was finished, Bouchard took a long swig of his beer and licked his lips. He chuckled and grabbed his laptop to work on a document about the impending purchase of a real estate complex in Mont-Tremblant, north of Montreal.

"Wow. What were the odds, man?" the slender guy said cheerfully after a few minutes.

Bouchard looked at him quizzically. The odds of what, exactly? The man pointed to the table with his chin. Bouchard looked around to see what he was talking about, noting that his boarding pass was exposed on the table.

"You're 3F. I'm 3D," the man said, showing him his own boarding pass.

Usually, Bouchard wouldn't care who was sitting next to him in business class, but he had to concede that it was indeed a weird coincidence.

"If we are to sit next to each other, we might as well introduce ourselves," the man added, extending his hand, waiting for Claude Bouchard to say his name.

"Claude Bouchard."

"Pleased to meet you, Claude. My name is Michel Madison."

Bouchard pulled his hand off Madison's, rubbing it by reflex; Madison's hand was freezing. It must have been the beer he had just brought.

"Well, my friend," Madison said, looking at him with an inquisitive eye. "I feel like we are going to have a very interesting flight."

GET TWO FREE BOOKS

Get two FREE short novels from this author. Discover two of his book series by visiting Sebastyen's website.

Download them for FREE by subscribing to Sebastyen's newsletter by clicking on this link:

https://link.sebastyendugas.com/brevisbacklibrary

ABOUT THE AUTHOR

Sebastyen Dugas is an author from Montreal, Canada. He started his career as a journalist and then switched to a career in computer science.

Writing has always been a passion for Sebastyen for as long as he can remember. He loved to write for his own pleasure as well as contribute to blogs for other publications.

In his spare time, Sebastyen enjoys reading, photography and film. He loves to travel and has already visited more than twenty countries.

In the coming years, he wants to continue to travel the world, write more fiction and enjoy life.

You can reach Sebastyen on his website or on social media.

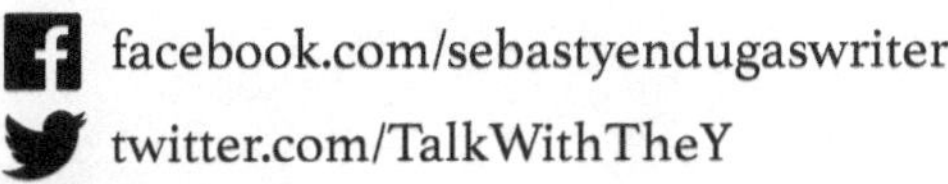

ALSO BY SEBASTYEN DUGAS

Abygaelle Jensen Series

The Wooden Queen

Martin Lafs Series

Epiphany From a Broken Camera

Don't Find Roger

Revenge is a Fish Better Served Cold

Brevis Series

Death Ride

Stockholm